BOOK TWO OF THE
REMNANT OF CHAOS SERIES

# REMNANT OF CHAOS II

## B. STORM

# Contents

# PROLOGUE

Roy Darsetts was a simple man. He had spent most of his life questioning how important he could truly be. He was nothing more than an ordinary office worker. He spent every waking hour in the confines of an office building known as the Archon Corporation.

But in the last couple of years, his life has changed drastically. He had met the woman of his dreams and even married her. She had been his protector, chosen by his brother. He still had no idea if his brother was even alive or dead. It is something that he has pondered for quite some time. He barely ever saw him anyway.

An alien race known as the Immortals viciously attacked him shortly after he met her. The Immortals are not stereotypical aliens but humans in disguise. They look nearly identical to us but bear supernatural strength. However, their mind is all but corrupted into the basic thought of bloodlust for violence and mindless destruction. He hadn't even realized it, but he had worked with one for at least a couple of weeks.

Everything changed for him on the day of his wedding. This is when his ordinary life went from boring to exciting in an instant. Even now he feared what may come next. But he knew that he had no choice but to accept this as his new reality. There was no telling what exactly he had gotten himself into, but he had accepted it as it was. Fortunately for him, he had discovered the weakness of the Immortals to be holy water. If he had not found out about this, he may very well have been brutally killed by his coworker. Now Roy and his friends carry weapons that can best the Immortals. He swore to kill them all for his wife's cruel death.

***

Just two months later, he had encountered two more Immortals. They had made his previous coworker seem like a joke in comparison. They each had turned into powerful demons before their inevitable defeat. Each of them had brought quite a challenging fight. But with the aid of his friends, Roy had managed to best them both.

Now he gripped the steering wheel in front of him as he remembered all of this. A lot has changed for him. He felt like nothing would ever be the same for him. The car seemed at least a decade ahead of any other car on the road. This car was vastly different on another front as well. The car is armed to the teeth with all sorts of gadgets and weapons. These devices had helped greatly in their fight with the Immortals as well as the demons.

A bald man was sitting in the passenger seat beside him. He glanced over at Roy.

"Are you alright, Roy?" he asked, sounding concerned.

This man had become his best friend when all this supernatural nonsense was thrust into his life. He had gotten Roy out of many life-threatening situations. He is Vince Stranglehan. At one time he was a wrestler, but after the arrival of dark and threatening forces, he had decided to become a soldier to help fight against them. There exists a secret society that fights against such threats. He had joined them without a second thought and has been helping them ever since.

"I'm just remembering all the shit that we've been through over the past couple of years," Roy replied. "It really has been a lot."

They still hadn't reached the Immortal who had coldly killed his wife in front of him. He was the one who had pushed Roy to make his decision to eradicate the Immortals. He had enough of their senseless killing. They needed to be stopped by any means necessary. He knew that once the one responsible was put down, he would continue hunting the Immortals until there wasn't a single one left. This was his quest for vengeance, and he knew that this was just the beginning. For there are many Immortals. The Secret Society that fought them has fallen, and they were all that was left.

"Just remember, Roy, we've got your back," a man said from the back.

He was sitting behind Vince, staring out the window with a blank expression on his face. There was a lot on his mind as he figured out what they should do next. But also, how would they fight the next Immortal that they came across? He is supposed to be even stronger than the last two Immortals that they fought. The Immortals hadn't been weak by any means. The man who was staring out the window was Phil Tyconian, a man who prefers shooting before asking any enlightening questions. His coat is riddled with a wide variety of firearms. All of which he uses depending on what the occasion may be.

"Not like we have much of a choice," a man said from behind Roy.

He was staring out his window, but his expression was anything but blank. It seemed to be a more annoyed expression. He is Derek Deathbed. He is an assassin who is very good at what he does. Sometimes he can be a bit much, but he has been a great help to all of them.

"You better not slow us down, Roy," Derek scolded.

"If I remember right, you got your ass kicked pretty good in the fight with the last demon," a woman said, smirking between the two men in the back.

"Don't know what you're talking about, Dedalia," he said.

Based on his tone, everyone knew that her words had struck him in just the right way. But he hid himself away behind his irritated expression.

"Just don't expect me to bail all of you out when the shit hits the fan. We have the chosen one for that shit."

"We'll see about that," she chuckled.

"What the hell is that supposed to mean?!" he questioned her angrily.

He had turned towards her amid his outburst. But she only smiled back at him. He hated it and returned to the view out of the window in disgust.

Dedalia was once an Immortal, as their enemies are, but she turned her back on their wicked ways. The people that she is with now are the ones that she believes in more than anything else. She knows that they will change the course of the battle completely. Destiny has plans for them on the planet that the Immortals call home. Unfortunately for the Immortals, the plans harbor a grim future for their continued existence.

***

There is but one more important person in this tale. He is far from the others on the planet where the Immortals make their home. This is a place known as Khais. He was not as comfortable as the others were in their car. He is bound to a pillar in the center of a library in the Demon Castle. His bonds were an enchanted chain aglow with a blue flame. He has already discovered that no matter what he may try, he will not be getting free of the chains. He has been here for as long as Roy has been on his journey through the supernatural. This man is Roy's older brother. Michael Darsetts.

This is the consequence of him trying to keep Roy away from the supernatural threat. In the past couple of years, things had escalated much worse than he could have ever imagined. He hated the fact that he hadn't been able to do anything to stop it. Now he was stuck here listening to a blue demon who seemed to have control over Roy's fate. Perhaps even his destiny could be at stake. He was so close to wiping out the forces of Chaos for good. This is what he had to show for it.

The demon he had been searching for was standing in front of him, holding an open book. He claimed that everything he read from his book were the very things that Roy had been going through while Michael had been busy trying to keep the darkness away from him. This demon is called the Tomekeeper. The demon looked to be quite frail but had powerful magic in his possession, making him quite a threat to him. He was rather surprised that the blue fire hadn't already burned through his clothes. Perhaps another aspect of the demon's magic.

He didn't want to trust the Tomekeeper but didn't have much of a choice either.

Michael tried to play it off as if he wasn't paying much attention to the demon as he spoke, but he hung onto every word. The more he heard about Roy's suffering, the more he felt the need to break free of the damned chains. He just needed the Tomekeeper to slip up and tell him something that he could use. Once he was free, he would kill this demon and find his brother.

Michael was rather surprised that Roy and the others had managed to best so many Immortals in as little as six months. It had started with a man who disguised himself as Roy's coworker. Then shortly after, they took out the mighty Parallax and finally Alioth. He had to admit he was very impressed. He wasn't sure if Roy would be able to pull it off. Roy was always the more emotional of the two. After hearing all this, he couldn't stop himself from letting a small smirk curl up onto his face. Of course, the Tomekeeper took notice of this.

"Does something amuse you, human?" The demon asked, bewildered.

"You have no idea of the shit that you have gotten yourself into," Michael responded with a wide grin on his face. "You may see my brother as insignificant, but now he has a purpose. You gave him the push that he needed. You have underestimated him, and that is why you will fail. Your precious allies are falling one after the other. I only wish that I could witness as your brethren are slowly slaughtered."

The Tomekeeper countered his idiotic grin with a crooked smile of his own. Michael didn't like the fact that the demon wasn't deterred in the slightest. The demon didn't even seem bothered by the death of his fellow demons. The whole thing made him feel rather suspicious. It just didn't feel right.

"This is just the beginning, Michael," the Tomekeeper replied nonchalantly. "The story gets so **much** better. Sure, a handful of my friends have perished, but you will soon experience some losses of your own. You should never rush the story. So, strap into those chains and enjoy the ride, human."

Michael processed everything that the Tomekeeper had just told him and felt a bead of sweat trickle down his forehead. This couldn't be real. He was beginning to feel anxious about how things would go next. He only hoped that nothing would happen to his dear little brother. He picked out his protectors as the best ones to be able to do so. But if they fell, everything and everyone would be doomed. It was not something that he had ever thought of as a possibility.

The Tomekeeper was still smiling at him. He knew that the demon was enjoying this. Being trapped by his greatest foe with him lying in wait directly in front of him is absolute torture. All he could do at this point was plot how he would kill this demon once he was free of these chains.

"You're looking nervous, mortal," the Tomekeeper said, smiling.

"Shut the hell up!" Michael barked at him. "Once these chains fail you, I will take your fucking head clear off your shoulders!"

"Struggle all you like," the demon cackled. "You will never be free of those chains. I made sure of that."

"Fuck!" Michael screamed in frustration.

His scream echoed off the walls of the library, while the demon just laughed at his anguish. He savored Michael's suffering. He enjoyed every second of it. He was eagerly awaiting just how much worse it would become for him.

# CHAPTER 1

# IMMORTAL DESPERATION

Due to the events of the Immortal's attack on New York City only a couple of weeks ago, there is an armored semi lying broken and useless at the bottom of the sea. Not too far from this sunken truck is an impossible sight. A mansion sits untouched on the seafloor. Its exterior is covered in moss, but apart from that, it appears to be in pristine condition.

There is a fence barring the way to the front door. Surely it would serve no purpose at the bottom of the ocean. It was a strange sight for anyone who would ever come across it. The insides of the mansion open upon what looks like an ordinary mansion with no sign of the water surrounding it ever leaking inside. Everything looked neat and organized.

The deepest point in the mansion holds an office. Inside the office, a man sat behind a desk, hunched over a basic laptop. The desk seemed to match the ornate feel of the place. The office's walls were lined with numerous bookshelves, each brimming with books of varying sizes. At least two statue heads stood upon two separate pedestals in the confines of the room. The statues seemed to stare at each other from across the room.

The man behind the desk is sporting a dark leather jacket and camo pants. His buzz-cut hair is an ashy gray. His face is focused on what he is seeing on the small screen of the laptop. He is one of the only Immortals to even get his hands on a laptop. He was only so lucky because he had searched one out when he surveyed Earth about six months ago. He preferred to be prepared. He always had plans and hated it when they went awry. This is the General. He is the one who killed Roy's wife in front of him. The one responsible for kickstarting Roy's quest for vengeance in the first place.

The General squinted at the screen and tried to wrap his head around the information that he was seeing. He hadn't expected both the Sergeant and Lieutenant to fail him. But what he was seeing now showed that the two of them had been killed. It didn't make sense. It should be impossible. Mortals are weak, feeble creatures, and yet they had destroyed some real monsters. Even with the traitor Dedalia among them, it shouldn't have been possible. Still, if he hadn't put those trackers on them, he never would have known of the deaths of his two allies. Still, he just couldn't fathom it. He was beginning to wonder if he should be worried about his own fate.

He clacked at the keys of the laptop more intensely, but the outcome stubbornly refused to change. This meant one thing. He would have to call him. But he was dreading this moment. The Commander would have to know what was happening. The General knew that he would not be happy. He was not looking forward to it but knew it needed to be done.

He slammed the laptop shut, and the desk crumbled in front of him, showing his own level of anger at the loss of his mostly reliable friends. He scowled before getting up out of his chair. The structures on Earth sure were fragile. He wandered over to the window and gazed out at the sea. This was not something he would be able to do on his home planet. Khais didn't have much to be desired in terms of oceans. Gazing upon the multitude of marine creatures gliding before him provided him with a sense of tranquility.

The General took a few deep breaths and contemplated how Roy had managed to pull off the impossible. He knew that Roy and his friends would be coming after him next. He would have to be ready. He didn't plan to go down easily, but still, he would need to be ready for things to go off the rails. He would beat this group of mortals no matter what. He needed to warn the Commander regardless.

He fished the phone out of his pocket and dialed the number to reach the Commander. His voice came out of his phone in response.

"General," the Commander said. "You better not be backing out now."

The General could hear from the harshness of his tone that the Commander was not pleased. He would just have to do his best not to antagonize him any further.

"I have some news," the General said rather reluctantly.

"Well, what is it?" the Commander asked impatiently.

He knew that there was no easy way to tell this to the Commander. So, he just went for it.

"Everyone is dead," he sighed.

"Are you fucking kidding me?!" the Commander's voice burst through the phone.

The General pulled the phone away from his ear and brought it back after the ringing in his ears dulled.

"How could this happen?" the Commander pondered from the other end of the phone.

"Elliot was killed at Roy's wedding," the General told him. "Parallax died in the middle of the streets of New York, while Alioth was killed in front of his own tower."

"No, no, no," the Commander said in a panicked voice. "This can't be right. I was told that this was going to be easy. He promised me."

"Who?" the General asked, feeling suspicious.

"The Chaosbringer, of course," he replied.

"Hold up. You were given this job by the Chaosbringer? And you trusted him? You realize he is the most untrustworthy person on our planet, right?"

The Commander let out a deep sigh.

"I didn't have a damn choice," he uttered. He drew out the words heavily, and the General could feel his regret from his end of the line. "If I chose to refuse him, I wouldn't be talking to you right now, and he would surely be on his way to kill you as well."

"Do you even realize who the Chaosbringer is?"

"I am well aware of who he is and what he is capable of."

The Commander's voice sounded drained. Almost defeated.

"Then you understand that he is pretty much Chaos himself," the General said at his wits end. He could hear the terror in his own voice. "He is a fragment of Chaos' very soul. He's not up to anything good. Even the king, Barbatos, doesn't trust him, and for good reason."

"It was the only way, General," the Commander said dryly. "It looks like it's up to me to get us out of this damn mess."

"You would have been better off letting us all die. If we fail, we may even succumb to an even worse fate."

"You may be right," the Commander agreed. "Just slow them down, and I will finish them myself."

The Commander seemed to think that the General was going to die. Despite the overwhelming odds against him, he was determined to eliminate their foes. The Chaosbringer may win, but he would not let a weak race be his end.

"It seems I'm being forced to draw my final card," the Commander said. "I didn't want to do this, but it seems that I have little choice."

"What are you talking about?" the General asked.

He honestly had no idea what the Commander had up his sleeve. He wasn't even sure of what forces they possessed that could aid them apart from any other Immortals.

"I will release the monsters," the Commander declared. "They will tear those bastards apart."

"We have monsters?"

"Yes, we do," he said, his voice trembling. "To ensure our success, I will have to summon **him**. Just in the off chance that all the monsters are bested."

"Another secret?"

"If they fail us, I will summon Judgement."

"Judgement?" the General asked in bewilderment. "The ancient demon that we have sealed in the basement?"

"The very same," he replied. "We need to make sure that these mortals will never have a chance to come crawling back to us."

"Is everything alright, sir?" the General asked.

He had never heard the Commander sound so scared. It made him feel nervous as to what could come next. Still, they had to win. If not, then everything they know will crumble beneath them.

"Don't let me down, General," the Commander said quietly. "I expect nothing but the best from you when the time comes."

"You will have it."

Then he hung up the phone, knowing that no more words were needed. Roy would fall, and his friends would be close behind him. He knew full well that Dedalia would be the greatest threat to him. But he would deal with that when she showed up at his door. For now, he would prepare for their inevitable arrival.

***

The Commander sat at his desk, blankly staring at the wall across from him. He was in a state of disbelief at everything that had happened. Two of his most trusted warriors were dead. They died at the hands of mortals, whom he had always considered weak. The fact that they had figured out how to kill his kind made him incredibly nervous going forward. He couldn't fight the sinking feeling that, in due time, they would reach him, and he would be forced to fight them himself. He couldn't allow them to keep their momentum going. He would stop them.

He grazed his hand across the underside of his desk and found the small groove he was looking for. He pressed his finger against it, and a bookshelf to his left slid open like a large sliding door.

"It's time," he said to himself.

Then he rose from his chair with a grunt and walked through the newly opened doorway. He descended the spiraling staircase. Upon reaching the bottom, he entered a large and open room that seemed to be waiting for him. This is the place where he kept all of his secrets. This is the domain of his monsters, gifted to him by the Maker some time ago. He never thought he would have to rely on them like this during his lifetime.

He stepped inside and peered around the room. It truly was massive, seemingly without end. It appeared to be a large storage room, but the actual storage had been removed quite some time ago. He didn't even know how long these monsters had been down here for. He sacrificed many of his minions to take care of these creatures in secret so that they would never grow hungry; other than that, he had never paid them any mind.

He stopped at a large hangar door and pressed his hand against a touchpad hanging on the wall next to it. There was a shrill screeching noise as the door came to life and slowly rose off the floor. The light from outside the mansion seemed to penetrate the room and reveal all the monsters stowed away in it. The first thing that he saw was a group of what looked like twenty hunched-over people.

These entities were not human beings but rather something much more grotesque. Each one of them had a torn cloak flimsily wrapped around them. Their bodies were deformed and twisted, barely holding the cloak in place. Their hair was stiff and formed what looked like tree branches. Every one of them held a large gun in their arms. The guns that they wielded fired forth either knives or swords. It all depended on the model that they held in their hands. These abominations are creatures known as the Turka. They were crafted by the Maker, an Immortal who made a habit of creating strange and dangerous creatures. He is responsible for nearly all of the known monsters on Khais. The Turka ran past the Commander and out into the wilderness that only the planet could provide.

A tall, pale-skinned man wandered past him. He looked similar to the other Turka but was still vastly different at the same time. His body wasn't deformed like the others, but his branch-like hair remained. However, it was more natural and slicked back. His cloak fit around him snugly, and he wore ragged shorts. His beady black eyes gazed out into the lit-up horizon, and he marched forward. He had abandoned the guns that the others had with them. In their place is a pair of curved swords. He has no real name. He is simply the leader of the Turka. He never spoke but understood the human tongue quite well.

The next group of monsters began storming past him. If the Turka were frightening, then these creatures were even worse. They had the lower body of a dragon but the torso of a human. They carried large, scaly wings just as if they were miniature dragons. Their draconic bodies came in a wide assortment of colors. Each one of them could breathe fire. They could emit a simple fireball or a continuous intense flaming stream. These beings are the Dragizar.

The most intimidating among them approached the Commander. His scales are a shade of darkness, and he has a formidable physique. He glanced down at the Commander, making the Commander feel rather small. He judged the Immortal with his piercing gaze.

"Why now?" the Dragizar asked gruffly.

"That's not for you to know," the Commander said, hiding the fear in his voice. "Just do your damn job."

"As you wish," the Dragizar said in understanding.

The Dragizar walked towards the others.

"You know that you are already dead," he said, chuckling to himself.

The Commander knew he was right, but he didn't have time to worry about that right now. Although the mortals have already made their move, soon they would see just how terrifying they could be as well. He had already seen a glimpse of what the Chaosbringer looked like when he was angry. He would rather not see what he was capable of when he fully embraced his rage. He would do his best to stay on his good side.

Just one monster remained. He was the worst of the worst. The Commander would have to break his seal. Fortunately, a powerful sorcerer among their ranks taught him how to break his seal. The Commander feared the demon in front of him almost as much as the Chaosbringer himself. The monster before him is the ancient demon, Judgement. In fact, he is one of the last ancient demons left.

Reluctantly, the Commander wandered towards the back of the room. Judgement was suspended near a wall by powerful chains. The demon smiled as he saw the Commander approaching him. He was bound above a magic circle that gave off a luminous blue light. The chains did nothing to actually hold him. The magic circle was doing all the real work. The chains were nothing more than a backup in case the magic circle failed. However, his arms had been stretched out for so long, they would probably be too sore to do anything. Not exactly a guarantee, but a possibility.

Judgement towers over the Commander by at least a foot. His scales being a dark obsidian. He looked upon the Commander with crimson eyes. The curved horns atop his head are long and slender. But the thing that stood out the most about him was the large eye protruding from his chest. The eye blinked at him as he approached. The eye harbored the magic that Judgement possessed.

"Well, well, well, Commander," he smirked. "You must be quite desperate to come to me."

"Judgement," the Commander stated. "Things have changed."

"You mean to say that you underestimated the mortals," he replied. "I expected as much, but still, I'm not surprised."

"How would you even know about what's going on out there?"

Judgement chuckled. "Even in my current state, I have ways of getting information that shouldn't be known to me."

"So, you know why I'm here then?"

"Of course. Just know that I have but one condition."

"What is it?"

"Give me that bitch, Dedalia," he growled. "I have my own score to settle with her."

"If that's all it will take, you can do whatever you want with her."

Judgement licked his lips with a long, pointed tongue.

"Oh, trust me, I will," he said, grinning.

"You're a sick bastard, you know that?" The Commander said, feeling himself cringe at the demon in front of him.

"That's not something that you need to concern yourself with, is it? Free me, and I promise to take care of your enemies."

"Fair enough," the Commander replied.

The Commander produced a small knife and sliced the blade across his wrist. He held the trickling blood over the magic circle. His black blood slowly fell to the circle, and it began to fail. The blue light flickered and became an ugly red hue. Then the light went out altogether.

Judgement ripped the chains free of the wall in an instant. He could feel the numbness in his arms but walked up to the Commander. The Commander drew a key from his jacket and stuck it into his shackles and twisted it until there was a click. The shackles snapped apart and collapsed onto the floor in front of the demon.

Judgement gripped the long handle of a large axe standing next to him and hoisted it into the air. He looked over the axe, admiring it. It had been quite some time since he enjoyed the feeling of his axe in his hand.

"How I have missed this," he said excitedly with a wide grin spread across his face.

"Don't forget what the mission is," the Commander reminded him.

"Don't ruin the moment," Judgement said, scowling at him. "I will destroy your enemies. I'm not a demon who would disappoint."

"Looking forward to it."

Judgement slipped the axe into a holster held up on his back.

"I'll bet you are," he said. "But I assure you, I will do all the things that you are too chickenshit to do."

# Chapter 2

# Highway
# to the Bottom of the Sea

Roy had become relaxed because they were in a car that practically drove itself. Slowly he came to the realization of where they were. They passed by numerous destroyed buildings and debris scattered across the road. The car swerved around the rubble as it went. Construction crews worked tirelessly on the battered buildings around them. He recognized this part of the town. It had felt like it had been much longer since they fled from the wrath of a powerful demon known as Parallax. But it had been nothing more than a couple of days.

Parallax had been an incredibly large demon. He still wasn't sure how they had managed to beat him. Parallax had caused all this destruction in mere moments. Now this innocent city had fallen victim to his unfathomable power. Roy was beginning to wonder why they were traveling down a road that they had already been on. Had they somehow slipped past the General, and he had missed it?

Then the car turned and drove out onto a pier. They knew that this was the place where they had forced the Sergeant's truck out into the ocean. What they didn't understand was why they were even here. The car rolled down the boardwalk with no people to block its path. A grateful thought. They didn't need to put any civilians in a panic. It raced towards the edge, ready to launch itself into the sea.

"This again?" Roy wondered aloud. "Is this a new way to make us all think that we're gonna die?"

"There is something seriously wrong with this car," Vince commented.

"That is offensive," a voice said.

The voice belonged to the AI that served as the car's computer. She was like Siri but at the same time quite different. She might even be considered more sophisticated. She had named herself Dina.

"I could make you walk, Vincent," she said pleasantly but with a sharp tone.

"I'm sorry," Vince apologized.

"I will forgive you," she replied. "It is simple. He is beneath the waves."

"What?" Roy asked. "You expect us to breathe underwater? We can't exactly swim all the way there."

"Humans are so skeptical," Dina sighed. "Trust me. You will be fine."

The car flew off the end of the pier and changed shape as it soared through the air. It condensed itself into a small submarine. The wheels tucked into the undercarriage of the car, and propellers popped out in their place. The windshield became curved. Then the car broke through the surface of the water. It drifted gracefully through the ocean.

"Delkeg was way out of his time with this beauty," Derek said in disbelief. "This is fucking amazing."

Everyone agreed in a stunned silence.

"Thank you, Derek," Dina chirped happily.

They all looked upon the wrecked remains of what was once the Sergeant's truck. They passed by it, and the sea life swam past them.

"Looks like the bastard may have been closer than we thought this whole time," Phil said.

"Looks that way," Roy agreed. "But we won't be passing him by again."

Roy took a good look at the sea creatures peacefully swimming around them. He couldn't help but admire the tranquility down here.

"It really is pretty down here," Dedalia said in amazement.

"Yeah," Roy agreed. "We should consider ourselves lucky. This isn't something that most humans would ever be able to witness in their lifetime. At least not in a car."

Derek just stared out the window blankly, trying his best not to get wrapped up in all of this as the others were. The view was mesmerizing, but he only wanted to focus on one thing. They had a job to do, and when the time came, he had to make sure that everyone would live through the day. A lot was riding on all of this, and he wouldn't let a few fish distract him.

They navigated around a large rocky structure and saw the outline of something that shouldn't be possible on the seafloor. Roy blinked a few times to ensure he wasn't seeing things. It was a large mansion covered in moss. But when he opened his eyes again, it was still there.

"Is that a fucking house?" he asked in disbelief.

"Well," Vince said surprised himself. "You sure don't see that every day."

"Here I was thinking that I had seen it all," Phil remarked.

The car drifted down toward the mansion in the distance. It brought itself down onto the seafloor in front of a gate that circled the mansion. The propellers had been tucked back inside its frame, and the wheels were brought out onto the seafloor. The sea creatures around this place were much larger and more ferocious in nature. They seemed to be drawn to the place. It was rather off-putting.

Suddenly, everyone felt a jerk as the car shot forth in a burst of speed. They smashed through the gate, and it was sent spinning into the ever-expanding sea over their heads. But the car just kept getting faster as it approached the mansion's front door.

"Here we go!" Roy shouted.

The car smashed through the front door, and the door was tossed across the floor of a massive room. A man standing by a flight of stairs stepped onto the door, stopping it completely. Roy had been expecting the water to come rushing in behind them. But it remained outside as if blocked by an invisible force.

"Destination reached," Dina said.

Roy had been gripping the steering wheel so tightly he could barely even feel his fingers anymore. He felt as if his soul had left his body.

"No shit," Roy replied shakily.

"I am sensing a spike in adrenaline," she replied.

"If you're gonna pull something like that, warn us."

"Noted. Next time I will warn you before busting into our destination."

"I would appreciate that."

Roy ignored her as he saw something that he had a difficult time believing. They had done it. They had finally reached **him** after all this time. The General was in front of them, standing on what remained of the front door to this place. The General was smiling at them. Roy clambered out of the car as quickly as he could, and Derek finally noticed him. He shook his head in disappointment.

"Well, this should go well," he replied.

# CHAPTER 3

# THE GENERAL

Roy had noticed the General as soon as the car had stopped and was in the process of crawling out of the car before anyone had the chance to stop him. Derek had never seen him move so quickly. In seconds he was out of the car and running at the General. He had finally found the man he had been searching for all this time, and he refused to let him get away.

He got within distance of the General and hurled a punch at his face. The General caught his fist easily. Roy could feel the sheer power radiating off his hand. He wasn't sure what he had gotten himself into and could feel his body begin to tremble slightly.

"I see that you have learned nothing," the General said.

A loud cracking noise reverberated throughout the room as the General crushed Roy's hand in his own. Roy screamed in pain as an intense sensation flared up through his arm. Then the man in front of him smashed his fist into his chest. Roy soared backwards and flew past the car. He crashed into a thick stone pillar and dropped to the floor unconscious.

Vince got out of the car and slammed the door shut behind him, and Dina chirped at him angrily. He didn't care. Anger had consumed him. He stormed towards the General with an intense fire in his eyes. Derek and Dedalia got out of the back, knowing that getting in his way now would be foolish. They would have to help the best that they could. However, they had never seen him so angry. Phil remained in the car and began assembling a gun to help with their current situation.

"You're gonna regret that, you piece of shit!" Vince bellowed.

"I don't think I will, big man," the General replied, unworried.

Derek swung his door open and hid behind it. He drew his pistols and was ready to use them once he had a clear shot. When he had the opportunity, he would fill the bastard full of holes.

The General brought forth a pistol and aimed it at Vince's face. Still, Vince wasn't backing down.

"If I have to, I will toss my life aside without hesitation," Vince said. "I'm not important. Roy is the important one. I'm simply the one helping him reach his goal."

The only reason the General hadn't shot him was that he was surprised by his tenacity. Vince stopped in front of him and glared down at him.

"Such a foolish notion," the General replied. "I haven't met anyone with so much courage in my lifetime. And that's a long fucking time, so that's saying something."

Vince grabbed the wrist of the hand holding the gun and twisted it. The General winced and dropped the pistol to the floor. Then Vince fiercely punched the General in the face. He staggered back, and Vince swung another punch into his already battered face. He staggered sideways, clenching his jaw. Then he countered with a punch of his own that connected with Vince's stomach. Vince reeled forward, and the General grabbed the back of his shirt. He hurled him against a pillar, and Vince dropped onto the floor. The pillar had nearly crumbled from the impact.

Derek had seen enough and fired at the General from behind his car door. The General rushed behind a pillar. He was fortunate that none of Derek's bullets had reached him. Now they ricocheted off the pillar he hid behind. Dust filled the air as bits of stone rained onto the floor. Normal bullets usually weren't an issue for him, but he knew the kind of bullets that Derek was shooting were special. The kind that could **actually** kill him. He needed to think of something, and fast.

The General noticed a statue head nearby. He took a deep breath and ran towards it. A single bullet dug into his shoulder, but that wasn't going to stop him. He lifted the stone head off its pedestal and chucked it at Derek. Derek had seen the statue head whizzing towards him.

"Shit!" he shouted.

He turned away from the window and lifted his arm as the statue shattered the glass behind him. The stone head collided with the back of his head, and he fell unconscious onto the floor. The General hadn't had such a challenge in some time, and his breathing increased in excitement. He gave a slight smile at everything that was happening. This was much better than being cooped up in that office. But then he felt a strong hand grip the back of his head.

He had hoped that Vince would have been rendered unconscious. He wasn't so lucky. What a bother. Vince smacked the General's face against the pedestal that the statue head had been sitting upon. He smashed his face against it until it crumbled.

The General blindly kicked behind him, and his foot went into Vince's gut. Vince was launched into a bookshelf behind him. He fell to the floor and weakly reached for the wall next to him. With difficulty he managed to slowly rise to his feet. He could already feel his consciousness beginning to fail him.

The General turned towards him. He could feel black blood running down his face. His face was contorted into a grotesque snarl.

"I grow tired of these fucking games!" he shouted. "It's time for your end!"

He began striding towards Vince with one thought in his mind. He would kill this man, and nothing would stop him. But then a hand gripped his shoulder. He glanced over his shoulder, not entirely seeing the person behind him.

"What now?!" he yelled in frustration.

Dedalia had gripped his shoulder. She had made sure the others were okay before she had made her way over to the General. But knowing that they were fine was all the assurance that she needed. Now she flung the General behind her, and he slammed against the floor. He slid but hit the floor so hard that he was propelled into the air and spun against a pillar. He collapsed onto his knees, with a hand hitting the floor in front of him. He looked up at her with rage dancing in his eyes. Then he glanced to his right and saw that the car that the heroes brought with them was practically right next to him.

He rose to his feet and smiled at Dedalia. "Looks like you left your guard down."

He turned towards the car and sprinted towards it. He knew that Phil was still inside and that he would make an easy target. Dedalia let the man run towards the car, knowing that Phil was almost finished setting up the gun he would unload on the monster. Still, Phil didn't like the look of the madman running towards him.

"I've got you now, mortal," the General cackled.

There was a final click as the last piece went into place. Phil was holding a bazooka in his hands. He awkwardly kicked the car door open and fired a rocket at the General. The rocket exploded into the Immortal's chest, and he was hurled backwards. He smashed through a window and drifted out into the sea.

"We're not done yet," Vince said. "We're not sure what he will do next, but I'm sure that now he will be an entirely different person."

Vince looked around nervously, hoping that he would be able to spot the General before he made his way back inside. He hadn't realized how close he was to a window, and it shattered. The General rolled towards him as Vince turned to face him. He vaulted onto his feet and gripped Vince by the throat, squeezing tightly. Vince could feel the need for air rising rapidly. He grabbed the General's arm in a desperate attempt to pry it free. But he lost consciousness before he had the chance and fell to the floor.

"Son of a bitch!" Dedalia screamed.

She ran at him and swung a fist at his face. He dodged her with ease and jabbed a fist into her stomach. She reeled forward but then countered with a mighty punch of her own in his chest. He was thrown through the wall behind him and slid across the floor of his dingy office. Dedalia casually opened the door of his office and stepped inside. The General grunted as he clambered back onto his feet.

He looked down at himself and realized how ridiculous he looked. The explosion had all but destroyed his jacket. He sighed and removed his jacket. A large hole in his shirt stood out in its center. His chest was severely burned. His weakness to flames proved to be quite inconvenient.

"So will you kill me now?" he asked. "And take away Roy's crucial moment?"

"What are you even talking about?!" she asked, annoyed.

"If you kill me, he won't be able to get his precious revenge on the man who coldly killed his wife in front of him. The only thing that motivates him. Will you really take that from him?"

"You can play your mind games all you like, General. But they won't work on me."

"No?" he asked. "A pity."

"I know that nothing would make him happier than knowing that you are dead. After all the shit that you put him through."

Her hands balled into fists, thinking about all the things that the General had put all of them through. The man is sickening.

"I think you're wrong, girl. Nothing would bring him more satisfaction than killing me himself. Thinking anything but is mere delusion."

"You speak as if you know him," she replied.

"Do I not?" he asked. "Are all mortals not the same?"

"You don't know shit about any of us. The fact that you call us mortals proves it."

The General chuckled. "I see that you have fallen hard for them, Dedalia. No wonder you blindly switched sides to be with them. Too bad that you will die alongside them."

There was more that she had wished to say to him, but then Roy rushed past her. He held the hilt of his blade in his hand and pressed the button as he reached the General. The blade shot through his chest and pierced through his back. His red blood dripped onto the floor. He felt a pain that he had not experienced in a long time. He smiled and then began to laugh loudly.

"How foolish of you, mortal!" he declared. "You may as well have dug your own coffin!"

Roy retracted his blade with a look of disbelief on his face. The General's body began to writhe violently in front of him. His body changed shape as the monster within him began to take form.

# CHAPTER 4

# SERVISUS

Dedalia had seen this change happen twice already with the two other Immortals they fought on Earth. Although the second one wasn't technically on Earth but in a pocket of Khais itself. Both Parallax and Alioth had done this after their vessels had been broken. However, for Roy, this was a very new experience. His face was stuck in a look of mortification. She was worried he may even get in the way at this point. She would have to ready herself in the off chance that he froze.

The General's flailing body began turning gray, becoming a scaly texture. His hands twisted into large claws, while his now barbed feet tore through his shoes. Large, curved horns grew out from the top of his head. His eyes stared through them in a piercing blue. He had a major difference from the other demons that they had fought. A large pair of scaly wings unfolded from his back. He was a little taller than Alioth had been, but nowhere close to the behemoth that was Parallax.

"Finally," he said. "Now I am free to unleash my fury on this pathetic planet."

"W-W-Who are you?" Roy stammered.

"Hmm?" the demon asked him. "You wish to know my name?"

He bent down towards him to get a better look at Roy's face. Roy could feel sweat trickling down his face. He was able to embrace his anger when facing the General, but something about this demon gave him only fear. His aura was absolutely intimidating.

"You may call me Servisus," he said. "However, you probably won't live long enough to remember it. Those two demons you fought before are nothing compared to me."

"You know you don't have shit on Parallax," Dedalia said coldly.

He turned towards her with an ugly look on his face. Then he turned back towards Roy.

"Excuse me for a moment," he said. "I need to have a chat with this bitch."

Roy wasn't sure how to respond as Servisus turned back towards her. Servisus shot himself off the floor and tackled her into the air. The two of them smashed through a wall, and he lifted her up into the air limply in his hand. Then he whipped her into the front of Delkeg's car.

The car chirped angrily as Dedalia's body dented its front end. Roy ran out of the office and stared up at the demon. He had no idea what the demon was capable of and didn't want to find out either. He needed to do something. He knew that this was just the beginning of his quest for vengeance. He was sure to find far worse monsters than this. He just needed to accept that. He would have to steel himself against this demon and show him exactly what he was capable of.

But then it dawned on him. Nothing had changed. This monster was the enemy. The same monster that was the root of his suffering. This was the time to make him pay. Roy's face went from scared to serious in an instant.

"You may look different now," Roy said. "But you are still the son of a bitch who took everything from me. I will make sure the suffering you gave me will be returned to you infinitely."

Servisus stared down at him and chuckled. "Is that right?" he asked, clearly amused more than anything.

Roy drew a pistol from his jacket and pointed it at the winged demon above him. "Lyn was the only good thing I had in my life, and you tore her away from me. Now it's my turn. I will tear you apart, you hideous abomination."

Servisus looked down at him, still smiling. "I look forward to it, you feeble little man."

He launched himself down to where Roy stood. Roy shot the demon twice before it reached him. The demon's claws sank into him, and he cringed in pain. The jacket didn't even stop them in the slightest; they still pierced right through. He was lifted into the air, and the claws were forcibly yanked out of his body. He spun through the air and crashed into a bookshelf. The heavy textbooks buried him under their weight.

Servisus glanced to his left and saw that Vince had regained consciousness. He was twirling his axe in his hand.

"You sure got ugly," Vince said in a mocking manner.

"All of you will die here, and my master will finally be able to live without having to look over his damn shoulders!" Servisus snarled. "You are nothing to me!"

"None of us will die here," Vince replied. "We will beat you, and then we will beat your master too."

"What makes you so confident?" the demon asked quizzically.

"We mortals may be weak in your eyes, but the good guys always win, while evil is always returned to ash."

Servisus' face twisted into a dangerous look. Vince knew that he was driving him insane. In fact, he was counting on it.

"Come and prove me wrong then, demon," he gestured.

Servisus screamed in anger and shot at him like a rocket. Vince ducked underneath him and turned towards the demon soaring past him. He swung his axe up into the demon's wing. It sliced through the scaly surface, and blood splattered over him. The demon spun through the air and slammed onto his right knee. Blood ran down his wing as he furiously glared at Vince.

"Wrong move," Servisus said in cold and quiet anger. "Your miserable life is still in my hands."

He launched himself at Vince once again, but this time, he reached for the handle of the axe. He gripped the handle and tugged it roughly. Vince strained against him, but Servisus managed to pull it out of his hands. He slashed his clawed hand against Vince's chest, and Vince was thrown against a wall. Servisus chucked the axe after him, and it lodged into the wall directly above his head. Vince exhaled with a sense of relief. If his aim had been slightly better, he would be dead right now.

"I can't believe you threw a rock at me," Derek said from behind the demon.

It seemed that now he was up on his feet as well. Such an annoyance. Servisus slowly turned around to face him.

"Do you truly think you can handle me all by your-self?" he asked.

"I'm not alone, and I think you know that," Derek replied. "Some of us may be out of commission, but we will be back and strike you even harder. I'll just keep ya busy until they are able to rejoin the fight."

Servisus couldn't help but chuckle. He was delu-sional. "So now you believe that your friends will be able to save you. No. No one is able to survive against my insurmountable fury."

He lunged at Derek and glided towards him. Derek was ready for him. He had drawn the hilts from his jacket and pressed the emblem as the demon had reached him. The blades fired through the demon's chest and poked out his back, narrowly missing the wings. Servisus let out an ear-piercing shriek, declaring the pain he was in. Derek pressed the buttons again to bring the blades back to him.

Servisus thrust his claws into Derek's chest and lifted him up into the air. It hurt to fly up into the air, but he endured it. He would make sure to crush this human he now carried. Then he whipped Derek back down to the car below. He crashed through the windshield of the car, getting a shrill chirp from it in response. Servisus pain-fully flapped his wings, holding himself in place.

Derek was in the front seats; he had been draped over them, lying on his stomach. Then he heard Dina's voice fill his head. "Initiating revenge mode."

Derek smiled at this. He wasn't sure what it would entail but knew it wouldn't bode well for Servisus. The top of the car slid open and formed a platform that Phil was conveniently standing on. He was standing behind a large turret that Derek was sure the car had graciously provided him. His feet were strapped to the platform to prevent him from sliding back from the recoil of the powerful firearm. He looked determined, maybe even excited, to use a gun of such a caliber.

"I've seen enough of your shit, Servisus!" Phil shouted.

He let loose a never-ending volley of bullets toward the flying demon. The demon did its best to veer out of the way of the infinite bullets. Many of them still dug into his scaly exterior. He spun through the air to better reach Phil. He tore Phil off the platform, the straps binding his feet snapping apart, and spun him against a pillar. Servisus began breathing heavily. It had been exhausting to navigate around all those bullets.

Servisus heard a clicking noise, and a spear had stabbed through his back. He howled in pain and glanced down below. Dedalia had stabbed him from the ground while he was distracted. She ripped the spear out of his back, and he was whipped through one of the windows. He drifted out into the ocean. Then he began screaming in pain.

Roy's eyes flickered open, struggling to believe what he was seeing. He climbed out from the heavy pile of books and stepped towards the broken window that Servisus was forced through.

"Stay back," Dedalia commanded. "We need to make sure he's dead."

Servisus was out in the ocean, a school of sharks of varying sizes feasting on his body. He didn't blame him for screaming. He couldn't even imagine what that must be like. He felt himself growing weak and fell against the car that had brought them here. Servisus was flailing around in a desperate attempt to get the sharks off him.

But then a thick cloud of blood formed in front of the horrific scene, and he could no longer see what was happening. He didn't have a good feeling about this. Then a burst of water rushed into the mansion through the broken window. The force that shielded the mansion from the invading water appeared to have fractured. A large great white shark slid across the floor of the mansion. It flopped off the floor and soared towards him. He ducked, and it flew over the car and crashed into the pile of books that had buried him just a moment ago.

Then another splash of water billowed into the mansion. Servisus had returned in a bloody mess. The sharks had done a real number on him. It was impressive that he was still alive. His large wings hung uselessly at his sides. Roy could feel his eyes locked on him in a hungry way. They seemed to hunger for his very life.

"Roy Darsetts!" Servisus shouted. "I will fucking kill you!"

Roy drew his pistol back into his hand and pointed it at his weakened adversary.

"Not if I kill you first, you son of a bitch," Roy replied quietly with anger.

Servisus screamed in his fury and ran towards him. Roy gripped the hilt of his blade, still in the confines of his jacket, as he shot the demon repeatedly. The bullets were unsuccessful at slowing the demon down, but Roy had hoped for it to reach him. As Servisus reached him, Roy pressed against the hilt, and the blade shot through his back. The demon coughed up his blood onto the floor next to Roy. Then Roy retracted the blade, and the demon collapsed heavily onto the floor into a pool of his blood.

Servisus crawled along the floor rather pathetically with his blood soaking the wet floor beneath him. He sunk his claws into the wet floor and attempted to shakily get back up. Roy turned towards him with a soulless look in his eyes.

"I don't think so, asshole," he said coldly. "Not after all the shit you put me through."

Roy strolled over to him, and as he stood over Servisus desperately trying to stand, he pressed the button on his hilt. The blade sprang out and pierced the back of Servisus's head. Servisus fell back to the floor with an awkward thud. His blood seeped into the floor all around him. Then his body began to decompose as the other demons had. In a few seconds his body had become nothing more than flecks of ash floating atop a puddle on the floor.

Roy allowed himself a small smile as he realized he had done it. He had beaten the bastard who had killed Lyn. She had served as his light in this dark and cruel world. She would have been Lyn Darsetts if she had lived, and they would have been as happy as can be. Finally, she could rest in peace. She would be free of worry as to what has become of the cruel world that they have come to know.

# CHAPTER 5

# JOURNEY
# TO ANOTHER WORLD

Derek crawled out of the wreckage of the windshield and saw what Roy had accomplished.

"Damn, Roy," he said, impressed. "That was pretty badass. How's it feel killing the bastard you were looking for?"

Roy looked down at his hands and saw that they were trembling. He put his weapons away before he had the chance to drop them. He became acutely aware that his breathing had grown heavy.

"I don't know," Roy said shakily.

"Shit," Derek said. "It kinda just hit ya, huh? I just killed my first guy, sort of feeling. I remember that like it was just yesterday."

"Maybe?"

Derek sighed and hung his head. "Yeah, that's exactly what this is."

He climbed off the hood of the car and approached him. He could see the tears welling up in Roy's eyes. He grabbed his shoulders and looked at him with the utmost seriousness.

"Look. You know you had to do this. But don't forget you've got a helluva lot more killing to do, kid. This is just the start of what you promised. So, you better step the fuck up and get used to it. Got it?"

Roy embraced him in a tight hug and sobbed against Derek's chest. Derek hung his arms at his side as Roy cried all over his jacket.

"Well, this certainly isn't how I expected this to go," Derek said, sounding unsure of how to handle the moment.

Roy didn't know what had come over him. Normally, Derek wasn't the person he would go to in this situation, but he was closest to him at the time. He felt that he was in denial over his wife's death. Somehow in the back of his mind he had thought that killing the General would bring her back in some way. But he was cruelly reminded of just how alone he truly was. She wasn't coming back no matter how much he wished for it. He could beg and even pray, but he knew nothing would happen.

Roy pulled away from Derek. He realized his actions may have seemed a little over the top.

"Sorry," he apologized. "Don't really know what came over me."

"You tell anyone," Derek warned. "I will fucking kill you."

"Always knew you were an emotional bitch," Dedalia said, wandering over to them. She was smirking in Derek's direction.

"Shut up!" Derek shot back.

"So, the cold-blooded killer has a heart in there after all," Vince said as he stood beside them. He was wearing the same stupid smirk on his face.

"Keep this up and I'll leave all of you down at the bottom of this fucking ocean!" Derek shouted.

Phil lumbered over to them.

"You gotta smart remark too?!" Derek inquired angrily.

"I don't give a shit," Phil remarked. "I'm more worried about what our next move will be."

"Good point," Vince said. "After all, our enemies on Earth are now all dead. So, what's next?"

"I know the General was nothing but a simple pawn," Roy grimaced, balling his hands into fists. "Let's take this shit to the son of a bitch in charge."

"Well, look who grew some balls," Derek said, smiling. "I'm on board."

"You realize what you're doing, Roy?" Dedalia asked.

"I know what I'm doing," he replied. "I'm gonna find the rest of the Immortals and kill them one after the other. Maybe they will even begin to fear me as they do my brother."

"Those are big shoes to fill, Roy. But if you are sure, then who am I to stop you? Just know that there will be no coming back. You will make yourself known to all the Immortals. You will encounter some of the most ruthless, bloodthirsty aliens in the universe."

Roy cracked his knuckles and took a deep breath. "I **will** keep my promise to Lyn. I will do everything that I can to make sure that the Immortals learn their place."

"Then there's only one thing left to do," she said. "We will go to them. Their planet is vastly different from our own. Things that are possible here are quite impossible there, and vice versa. You got a small taste of that at the Lieutenant's tower. So, are you ready?"

"They have an entire planet?" he asked.

"Of course. What other place would be able to harbor such vast numbers?"

Roy remembered what Delkeg had told him the last time that they had seen each other. A man who had armed them with the very weapons capable of defeating the Immortals. Delkeg had told him to wait to use the Portoball that he was given until the time was right. It was starting to make sense. This may be their best chance. There was nothing left for them here anyway. It was time to bring the fight to them. He fished the Portoball out of his jacket and fidgeted with it in his hand.

"Not yet," Dedalia warned. "We will need to all press our buttons at the same time. There's no telling where we could end up. Not to mention what could be waiting for us either. We must ensure that we each reach the same place."

Everyone brought out the Portoball that Delkeg had so graciously given them. Roy couldn't help but wonder how Delkeg was doing. He only hoped that nothing bad had happened to him. Roy rolled the silver orb in his hand as he pondered this. This would be a big step for each of them. They would be traveling to the planet that the Immortals called home, knowing that they might **never** return.

"Roy?" Dedalia asked, intruding on his thoughts. "Are you sure you're ready?"

"Let's do this," he said.

Each of them hovered their finger over their designated Portoball in anticipation.

"Alright, everyone, press your button when I give you the word," Dedalia demanded.

Roy wasn't really sure why she seemed to be in charge all of a sudden, but it still didn't bother him all that much. He looked around and saw that everyone else was waiting patiently.

"Now," she demanded.

They each pressed the button on the orb at the same time in perfect sync. It was almost as if they had rehearsed for this moment many times over. They vanished into the air and left the mansion behind under the raging waves of the sea. The place they had reached was something else entirely.

They were now standing on a dirt path stretching through a barren wasteland. The sky was thick with dark clouds, and the road they were on appeared to stretch on endlessly. The trees were dead yet still stood at the sides of the pathway. Everyone was brought back to reality as Derek loudly puked at the side of the path.

"I fucking hate teleporting," he groaned.

He wiped the vomit off his face on the back of his sleeve and could see them all staring at him like a circus attraction.

"What?!" he asked irritably.

"Aren't you just delicate?" Dedalia chuckled.

"Fuck off!" he shot back.

They waited a few moments for him to regain his composure, and then they began heading down the path before them.

"What is this place?" Roy asked.

"This is it," Dedalia replied. "Khais, the place that the Immortals call home."

"What an ugly place."

"There isn't much civilization here, so we wouldn't be able to make much of a city anyway. It's more of a mystical place. There isn't much else we can do given the presence of all the monsters and demons roaming its surface.

"Fair point. So, what's next? Just travel down this path?"

He felt raindrops begin to patter on his clothes. It started light at first, and then quickly it became heavy.

"At least it seems that the Portoballs brought us to the right place," Dedalia noted. "But this rain is really something else. First, we'll need to find some shelter. But it's incredible how many steps ahead that Delkeg was."

"What do you mean?" Vince asked.

She pointed at the structure at the end of the path. The building was difficult to see through the thick rain, but they could tell that it sat there patiently awaiting them.

"That's the place where the Commander is," she said. "He's the same one who sent those four after us on Earth."

"So, he's the one responsible for everything," Roy said. "What the hell are we waiting for?"

"It'd be best if we were prepared before rushing in. We don't know what monsters may lie in wait for us on this trail. A wide variety of monsters do call this place home."

"Well, I definitely don't wanna stand around here to find out."

"Just keep your eyes open. The monsters in this place can be quite nasty."

"How bad could it be?" Roy asked.

He hadn't even realized just how quickly he would regret his words. Derek cried out as a knife swished through the air and dug into his right shoulder.

"You were saying," Derek said, cringing in pain.

# Chapter 6

# Turka

Derek grunted, pulling the knife out of his shoulder. "You just had to open your damn mouth, didn't ya?"

He was about to toss the knife aside, and then he saw the strange creatures approaching them. Their hunched-over bodies cradled large guns in their flimsy arms. But then all of them, at once, pointed their guns awkwardly in their direction.

"Turka," Dedalia breathed in disbelief.

"Snap the hell out of it!" Derek demanded. "Take cover!"

Unfortunately, there weren't too many places to take cover in this desolate wasteland. Everyone hid behind a tree of their own as best as they could. They hoped that the trees would fulfill their intended purpose. They were about to find out. The Turka fired their guns, and blades of all sorts of shapes and sizes were fired through the air. The trees became victims of the raining blades.

Derek looked down and saw the bloody knife that was in his shoulder now lay dormant in the palm of his hand. Maybe he could use it to take down at least one of their attackers. He would have to wait for a break in their relentless assault.

Roy had barely made it behind a tree, and a blade stuck to the ground next to his foot.

"What the hell is happening?!" he asked in a panic.

His question could barely be heard over the loud clicking of the Turka's guns. The sound of them reloading their weapons was deafening.

"These are just some of the monsters that I was telling you about!" Dedalia shouted over the Turka's clicks.

"How are we supposed to fight back against something like this?!" Vince shouted over them.

"Just wait!"

"Wait? For what? Them to kill us as we sit here helplessly?!"

"Trust me!"

"Does it look like there is a fucking choice?!"

Vince shook his head in defeat. There was no real choice. It didn't mean that he had to like it.

Derek was in the same state of mind. He didn't want to have to wait for them to stop firing their guns, but it was simply too dangerous to come out from their cover. He was feeling antsy, knowing that one of them had shot him with a knife. He was all too eager to give him his knife back. He didn't often get stabbed, and he didn't want to make a habit of it. But then the loud clicking sound stopped. He peeked around the tree. The Turka had stopped reloading, but only because they had nothing left to reload. They clumsily walked towards any ammo that they could find.

"Now's our chance!" Dedalia shouted. "Take em out while we still have the chance!"

Derek smiled and stepped out from behind his tree. Then he chucked his knife through the air, and it sunk into a Turka's face right in between the eyes. It flopped over backwards onto the muddy ground.

"Looks like I still got it!" he exclaimed. "Which son of a bitch wants some next? Go ahead and step forward!"

Derek brought out his pistols and fired upon the encroaching enemy. Each shot struck them in the head, giving them an instant death. Phil fired a rocket past him, and it struck a group of Turka about forty feet away. The Turka were scattered across the wasteland. Most of the Turka were taken out by the explosion. Phil left the bazooka by the tree and drew a shotgun. Then he pumped shell after shell into the Turka that remained.

The others took out any Turka who managed to survive. Vince mowed them down with his machine gun, while Dedalia's rifle brought each one down with ease. Roy had to fire three bullets into each Turka. He had a harder time aiming his gun, as he was newer to this than the others. Also, his gun just wasn't as powerful as the others were. Things were starting to turn around for them. Or so it seemed.

A large Turka had made his presence known. He was tall and slender and brought another group of Turka with him. He held a curved blade in each hand. This is the leader of the Turka.

Dedalia couldn't believe her eyes. "I can't believe that son of a bitch is real."

"You've never seen this thing before?" Roy asked.

"Never!" she shouted over the now pounding rain.

"I'll take care of the big one!" Derek shouted.

"Are you out of your fucking mind?!" she screamed.

He looked back towards her, smiling. "Most of the time."

Derek holstered his pistols and brought out the hilts that would become swords. He pressed the emblems, and the blades sprang forth.

"Hey, asshat!" he shouted. "You and I are gonna fight! Then you are letting me and my friends go! You got it?!"

The leader cocked his head down at him curiously. It looked like it was in a mocking manner, and something about it just didn't sit well with him. The large Turka in front of him lifted up the sword in his right hand and pointed past Derek.

"Well, shit," Derek sighed. "That's not good."

Then the large Turka made a loud clicking noise with his mouth, and the Turka began firing the blades through the air once again.

"Damn it!" Derek shouted.

He saw his friends rushing to the trees as the blades flew through the air. Still, he knew he would be safe where he was for now. They wouldn't bring down their own leader.

"Great job, asshole!" Phil shouted from behind his tree.

"How was I supposed to know that he wasn't gonna listen!" he shouted back.

"If we get out of this shit, you owe us a round of beer back on Earth!"

"You could just be grateful I tried to save your ass!"

"Why would I be grateful?!" Phil asked. "We all could have died!"

Derek could hear the Turka's blades swinging through the air towards him. He turned toward the Turka and lifted his blades up against his enemy's curved ones. He admired the sleek sharpness of the blades of his enemy.

"Looks like that backfired," he said, looking around at the madness all around him.

His swords slid off the Turka's as he pushed the monster back.

"Alright, you ugly fuck," he said. "It's about time I made you pay for threatening my friends."

The leader just made a clicking sound and slashed his swords down at him, and Derek sent his own crashing against his. Their weapons clashed against each other for several minutes. Then he heard everything go quiet. The Turka ran out of ammo and were scrambling to pick it up. Derek was only distracted by it for a second, but the Turka leader took that chance without a second thought.

The Turka thrust one of his blades at Derek. He noticed it at the last second and tried to sidestep it. Unfortunately, the blade grazed his side, causing him to wince in pain. Still, he lifted his swords to meet the other blade as it came rushing down towards him.

***

Dedalia had run towards a tree, and a knife was fired towards her. She caught it in her hand and whipped it back at the Turka. The knife went directly into the Turka's chest, and he collapsed onto the ground. She slumped against a tree, trying to catch her breath, and a blade pierced the trunk next to her.

"Damn," she said, catching her breath. "I really wish these trees were sturdier."

***

Phil had left behind his shotgun and was now using a rifle to bring down the Turka one after the other. He had fired the rifle at them as he had run to a tree of his own. If it weren't for the heavy rain pouring on them, this would prove to be much more difficult. The blades whizzed past him as he ran. Then he noticed a sword coming directly at him. He knew he wouldn't be able to outrun it. He leapt through the air and splashed onto the muddy ground. The blade struck the ground next to his face. He sighed in relief. He crawled over to the tree nearby and sat against it. He took a moment to regain his energy.

"Never thought I would be so happy for the rain," he said to himself.

***

Vince pelted the Turka with a steady stream of bullets from his machine gun as he made his way to a tree not too far off. He reached the tree without incident. But then a blade burst through the trunk at his knees, in between his legs. Another burst through by his left side. He exhaled heavily. He couldn't believe how lucky he was.

"Fucking shit!" he shouted in disbelief.

Even though he was protected by cover, he still felt very vulnerable. He didn't like it one bit.

***

Roy ran to his tree, unloading bullets into the Turka as he went. He managed to kill one of the Turka, but not before a knife grazed the top of his shoulder. He winced as he could feel warm blood running down his arm. He reached the tree and slumped down against it. The raining blades slammed against the other side of the trunk as he caught his breath. He began to wonder if these were the simple monsters on this planet; the dangerous monsters must be on an entirely different level. Probably nothing more than servants to the Immortals. Quite the thought indeed.

***

Derek was straining against the one blade pressing against his two. He was beginning to feel winded, and he knew that it showed. Still, he would need to persevere. The others were depending on it. He looked up at the large Turka in front of him.

"Looks like you can fight," he said with effort. "But you aren't getting the better of me."

He did his best to sound tough. He needed to make it seem like he could pull this around into his favor. He was sure that the Turka hadn't even bothered to pay attention. The Turka made a clicking sound, and he could feel himself being pushed back. It had been toying with him this whole time. Now it was using its full strength. It was just ridiculous. Derek's feet slid back across the muddy ground. He glared up at the monster with fiery eyes.

"C'mon!" he screamed in frustration. "I can't lose here! Not now!"

The Turka made a swift movement, and the swords were knocked out of Derek's hands. They stuck to the ground next to him, and the monster stabbed his left blade through Derek's left shoulder. He had evened it out so that now both of Derek's shoulders had been wounded. This made Derek's swordplay for their fight nearly impossible.

"Shit," Derek said weakly.

The Turka jerked his blade free of Derek's shoulder, and Derek brought out a pistol in his right hand. It hurt like hell, but he needed to stop this thing. He shot it in the chest. Between the heavy rain and the fact that he could feel his consciousness slipping from his loss of blood, his sight was starting to fail him. He was feeling dizzy. He knew he had pissed off the large Turka. This could be the only chance that he got. He would make the Turka pay for what it had done to him.

Just then, the Turka began flailing wildly in front of him. He wasn't sure if he had done something to the creature in front of him, but he was alright with it in any case. Its blood began spraying into the air all over its body, and then it splashed onto the muddy ground in front of him.

A group of soldiers was standing behind where the Turka had once stood, holding machine guns in their hands. He understood now what had happened. A gray-haired man approached him. His baggy clothes were soaked by the pouring rain. He was cradling a shotgun in his hand, and a cigarette hung loosely from his lips. He placed his right foot onto the corpse in front of Derek and looked at him. He holstered the shotgun he had been carrying, and he cupped his hands around his mouth to better light his cigarette in the pouring rain. The man seemed thrilled as the nicotine rushed into his system. Then he seemed to look at Derek quizzically.

"Who the hell are you?" Derek asked, somehow still standing.

The look the man gave him seemed to be one of judgment.

"You're welcome," he growled.

Then the loss of blood and excruciating pain had gotten to Derek, and he passed out onto the muddy ground.

"Jesus Christ," the man sighed, shaking his head.

# CHAPTER 7

# SURVIVORS CAMP

Derek awoke in a rather shoddy bed. Looking around, there were a few other beds, but he was unsure where exactly he was. It appeared to be a massive tent. Dedalia was sitting next to him in a folding chair with her hand clasped in his. This whole time she must have cared more for him than he had thought. He honestly hadn't expected it. She looked to be quite worried.

He could tell that the people who had saved him had taken good care of him. So, he knew that they weren't bad people. But the question still lingered in his mind. Why? Or who are they, for that matter? He knew he should be grateful to them. They did save him and the others. They even seemed prepared for that tall, freakish monster that they had encountered.

He turned towards Dedalia and saw tears welling up in her eyes. So, she did care about him after all. After all the times that he had tried pushing her away, here she was, closer than ever before. He had no idea what he had done to deserve the respect of such a wonderful woman.

"Am I dead?" he asked.

"No," she replied.

He could tell she was fighting her emotions the best that she could, but they still made themselves known through the wall she mentally put into place.

"I assumed so. Normally you aren't so nice to me. In fact, I didn't realize you even gave a shit about me in the first place."

She punched him in the chest, and he grunted as more pain surfaced.

"Jackass," she said and stormed out of the tent.

He groaned as he sat up in the bed. A soldier was standing nearby with a machine gun saddled on his back. The soldier looked over at Derek, who was wearing a look of discomfort.

"She looked after you the whole time that you were here, you know," the soldier said. "Looks like she could mess you up just as easily."

"Do I know you?" Derek asked.

The pain began shooting through his body all at once. The healing process still needed some time, it would seem.

"Just what I've noticed," the soldier replied.

The soldier picked up a shirt off a nearby table and tossed it onto Derek's lap.

"Put that on. Don't wanna scare anyone else out of here, do ya?"

"I haven't scared anyone yet," Derek said coldly.

Then he noticed the bandages on his body. He knew that he was lucky to still be alive. There was a bandage wrapped around his side, and two others bound his shoulders. His wounds would make his continued work much more of a challenge. He would still continue the fight. He would just have to ignore the pain that was sure to make itself known. He winced as more pain seared through him as he put the shirt back on. He glanced over and saw the soldier staring at him.

"You get a good look?" he asked the soldier.

"You really should be nicer to people," the soldier said, rolling his eyes.

"Did I ask your fucking opinion?!" Derek shot back.

"You sure didn't," the soldier said and left the tent.

"Where the fuck is everybody?" Derek pondered to himself.

He grunted as he got out of the bed and grabbed the jacket that had been draped over the chair where Dedalia had sat. He knew she had been safeguarding him as he was healing. He slipped it on and sighed. She really is such a good person. He should apologize to her for being such an ass. Maybe next time that he saw her, he would. He took the weapon harness from the table near where his shirt had been and strapped it on. Then he picked up his weapons and slipped them into the harness.

He made his way out of the tent and saw everyone except for Dedalia. He wasn't particularly surprised. She would probably need some time before talking to him again.

"Have a good nap?" Roy asked.

"How long have I been out?" he asked.

"Two long and uneventful days," Phil said. "I suggested that we move on without you."

"Of course you did, asshole," Derek snarled.

Still, he hadn't imagined he would have been out for so long. A couple of hours he could understand, but a couple of **days**? They must have had a hard time saving him. The Turka leader really did a number on him.

"Dedalia wouldn't hear it, though," Phil commented. "She wanted to make sure that you were with us."

"She must really like me then," he said, smiling.

"Don't know why. You're kind of a dick."

"Fuck off, man."

"My point exactly."

"Can we stop bickering like children?" Vince asked. "We need to figure out where the hell we are."

"We should probably ask the guy in charge," Roy said. "If not for him, who knows if Derek would still even be alive right now?"

"I had that shit under control," Derek stated.

"Sure, you did," Phil said, rolling his eyes.

A pair of soldiers approached them. Roy nudged Phil in the rib, and he turned to face them.

"What is it?" Roy asked them.

"The Leader wishes to meet with all of you," the soldier on the right said.

"Lead the way."

The soldier nodded and guided the four of them through the campsite. They passed by several other tents, some barely in one piece. Others had wounded soldiers propped up against them. Regular soldiers tried to help the wounded, but they had no real medical knowledge, and it showed. There was a firepit near each tent, with soldiers huddling around it. They either tried to keep warm or scrounge up some edible food.

"What happened here?" Roy asked in bewilderment.

"It'd be best if the Leader himself explains it," the soldier in front of them responded.

They reached a large tent similar to the one Derek had been in when he was taken care of. At the front flap of the massive tent, another pair of soldiers stood guard. Dedalia was nearby, leaning against a tree. She gave Derek the coldest look imaginable. It made him shiver a bit, and the hair on the back of his neck stood up.

"Good of you to finally show up," she said with a lack of emotion, but she stared directly at Derek.

"Guess she's still pissed," Derek observed.

"Yep," she replied bluntly.

The soldiers in front of the tent stepped aside, and the five of them followed after them with Dedalia in the back. She still wanted to be as far away from Derek as she could get. But not so petty as to not know that she would need to hear what the Leader wanted to say to them.

The tent seemed to be just as gigantic on the inside as it had on the outside. Derek recognized the man who had saved his life at the back of the tent sitting in a folding chair. Two coolers sat on either side of him. It seemed he was the only one worthy of such luxury in this place. The man looked at them with a dead look in his eyes.

His gray hair is in a tattered mess, hanging limply in front of his eyes. He is wearing a heavy gray jacket and baggy pants. He took a heavy puff from his cigarette and flicked it aside.

"Are you this Leader that we've been hearing about?" Derek asked.

"Yeah," the gray-haired man said soullessly.

Derek then noticed the flask in the man's hand. The Leader uncorked the top and took a big swig of the booze inside.

"You wanted to see us?" Derek asked, trying not to judge the man in front of them.

"Indeed," the Leader said. His words were on the brink of slurring. He was at least buzzed from the alcohol.

He wiped his mouth on his sleeve and looked at them seriously. "I wanna know where in the hell you guys came from."

"Earth," Roy said, feeling it should be rather obvious.

The Leader took another swig from his flask. "What I want to know is **how**."

The deadness of his eyes switched to annoyance in an instant. "I've spent the past couple of years trying to figure out a way off this goddamned planet, and all of you just waltz in out of the blue. So, I need to know. How?"

"How did you get here?" Roy asked him.

"Avoiding the question with another question, eh?"

He tipped the rest of the booze from the flask down his eager throat. The emptiness dawned on him, and the disappointment crawled onto his face. It clattered across the tent floor as he tossed it aside.

"Why do you even care about how we got here?" he asked.

"Maybe we can help you?" Roy suggested.

"Help us? Don't tell me you took a one-way trip!"

"We used the Portoballs that we got our hands on," Dedalia reported.

"Let me guess," the Leader said, rising from his chair. He stretched his back, and a loud cracking noise echoed throughout the confines of the tent. "Delkeg, right?"

"Yeah," Vince said.

"Fuck!" he shouted in frustration. "Damn that son of a bitch!"

"Why does that mean anything?" Roy asked.

The Leader balled his hands into fists and glared at the group in front of him. "So, you really want to know what happened to us? With that stupid look on your face. You look as if you haven't seen the shit that this place offers, but still, you wanna know?"

He laughed but was still furious. He just couldn't believe these people who were brought to his doorstep. He could see Roy just looking at him and knew that he had hope. Damned fool.

"So be it," he growled. "It all happened during that battle with Chaos a couple of years ago. We were saved by a being who calls himself the Portalkeeper. He looks human but is something else entirely. He made us a portal, promising it would take us someplace safe. But the damned thing brought us to this hellhole. Now, I don't know if I'll ever see that pretty blue sky that I got to see every day during my time on Earth. Now all I ever have are these disgusting gray clouds over my head that follow me everywhere I go.

Most of my people have been killed over the years. I'm fucking done with this place. Either I find a way to go home and live as a peaceful hermit, or I hope that one of you will kill me, putting me out of my misery. So, there you fucking go. Now you know our damn story!"

"Feel better?" Derek asked in a mocking manner.

"Don't you fucking start with me!"

"We don't want any trouble," Roy said. "Just let us rest here, and we will be on our way in the morning. Our only real goal is to kill the Commander."

Dedalia felt that he really shouldn't have mentioned it. The expression that twisted onto the Leader's face all but confirmed that she was right.

"You probably shouldn't have said that," she whispered in Roy's ear.

"You're gonna kill the Commander?" the Leader questioned. "A greenhorn like you? What a fucking joke."

"I'm serious," Roy said. "He took someone important from me, and I'm on my way to make him pay the price."

"Yeah, yeah, sure. Go right ahead. Stay here. I don't give a shit. But once morning hits, get your asses out of here. I'm tired of looking at your hopeful faces. They're misguided. Once you're here long enough, you will understand. I'm done with you."

"We're leaving," Vince said.

Vince gripped Roy by the shoulder, and the five of them left the tent. The Leader lit up another cigarette and took a deep puff.

"I can't afford to share their sense of hope," he sighed. "I can't risk my hope being taken away. **Not** again."

Outside the tent, Roy and the others were heading in the direction of an abandoned tent. It was one of the few abandoned tents in the campsite. Most other tents were occupied by soldiers or the wounded.

"What is his problem?" Roy asked, fuming.

"I know, right?" Phil agreed. "He's more of a dick than Derek."

He glanced over at Derek, who was walking beside him. "No offense."

"None taken," Derek replied. "I know I'm a dick."

Dedalia nodded in agreement, and he knew she still wasn't over their confrontation from when he first woke up. Still, they continued onward and reached the tent that they were directed to. The soldiers had thoughtfully left them everything that they would need to get through the night.

Each of them nestled up into their own sleeping bag. Phil fell asleep almost right away while the others restlessly tossed and turned through the night. Phil pulled his sleeping bag around him more tightly as suddenly he felt a shiver. He had been fine a moment ago, but now his body seemed to just get colder. Then he was whisked away into the world of his dreams. It wasn't a normal dream by any means.

# CHAPTER 8

# THE MESSENGER

Phil could feel his teeth involuntarily chattering, as he just kept getting colder. But then his subconscious slipped away to someplace else entirely. He blinked his surroundings into focus. The whole place seemed unreal. He was standing in the center of a castle hallway that stretched on endlessly. In place of the walls was a thick layer of mist. The only thing he could figure was that he was in his own dream. It should be an impossible feat, but after everything he had seen over his time since joining the Secret Society, maybe it wasn't so impossible.

A man was standing in front of him. He has long, wavy brown hair. It was neatly styled as if he cared about how it was kept. The man gave off a sense of importance, but he wasn't sure just how important. He looked like he was an Immortal, with a leather jacket and torn jeans making up his attire. The man was smiling at him. It made him nervous because he felt that he had never met the man before.

"Who are you?" Phil asked. "And what is all this?"

"I don't have much time," the man said, the smile fading. "It seems that you were the only one I was able to reach. I am Alciel, Prince of Demons, and this is the realm of your dreams."

"The Prince of Demons?" he asked. "How the hell are you in my dream? And how am **I** in my dream?"

"Sadly, I don't have the time to explain it. Just know that I have entered your dream to warn you of what's coming."

"Why should I trust you?"

"Because no one is helping you more than I am," Alciel sighed, hanging his head. "I was the one who gave Delkeg that nudge to help you out. How did you think that he knew you were coming? I made Darkus aware of your arrival at the Lieutenant's tower. I'm doing everything to ensure you win the fight against the Immortals."

"I guess that's a start," Phil said with a scowl.

"I wanted to warn you about the Turka, but they had arrived sooner than I had anticipated."

"So how are you supposed to help us against what's to come?"

"You're not very trusting, are you?"

"Not really."

Alciel sighed deeply but then looked back up at Phil. "I think you will appreciate my warnings."

"We'll see," Phil replied.

Alciel shook his head in disbelief and snapped his fingers. His body disappeared into the mist, and something else spawned in his place. It was a horrific monster with the lower body of a dragon with thick scales of darkness. A slender and thorny tail swayed behind him. While his upper body resembled a bald man with rippling muscles.

"What the hell?" Phil asked, surprised.

"This is a creature known as a Dragizar," Alciel said, his voice echoing around him. "This one in particular has a fated link with your friend Roy."

"Friend may be a bit of a stretch," Phil said. "Just doing a favor for his brother."

"There is no need to lie to me," the echoing voice said. "I know how you truly feel."

"What do you mean?" Phil asked.

"Don't underestimate the power of your dreams," he said. "Your subconscious tells me everything that I need to know."

"My mind has always been my worst enemy," Phil replied, disappointed.

"It is crucial that Roy is the one to drive him off. His actions will change the grim future that lies ahead."

"Of course, just more bullshit being piled on his shoulders," Phil said, sounding quite annoyed. "All of you expect far too much from him."

"I know you don't like any of this, Phil. Just promise me."

"Fine. I'll make sure. I'm just surprised you don't want him to kill this thing. Won't it come back to haunt him?"

"It has to come back for him. It is what fate has decided."

"I don't give a shit about fate."

"I know. Most people don't. But fate cannot be avoided. Nor can it be changed. That's just how things are."

"If you are looking to those connected by fate, then why am I the one who is here?"

"The others couldn't be reached. So, I settled for you. But know that your fate will take its hold on you rather soon."

"What do you mean by that?" Phil asked. "Has fate chosen how I die or something?"

"Ultimately, that is your choice," Alciel said. "But everything will go much better if you make the proper choice. But yes. You will have to die."

Phil was stunned. All this time he had imagined himself reaching the end with the others. He was now being told he might have to die to ensure they made it to the end in his place. He couldn't even fathom it.

"But I don't want to die," he said, feeling tears welling in his eyes.

He had never thought much about death until now. Sure, he had killed many to get to this point. But the thought of actually dying tore at his heartstrings.

The Dragizar was lost to the mist. It turned into something else altogether. It appeared to be some kind of gate. It appeared as though it belonged in the depths of hell, adorned with a coat of blackness. The face of a demon was carved into its center. The eyes shimmered in a crimson glow reflected off the gems in their sockets.

"This is the Chaos Gate," the voice echoed around him. "This is the being that will take your life."

"I'm gonna die by a damn fence?" Phil asked in disbelief. "You're kidding me, right?"

"It is a much more dangerous structure than you could possibly imagine."

"And what if I decide that I want to live and say, 'Fuck this fence'?"

"Then your friends will succumb to a cruel fate."

Phil scratched his head nervously as he pondered this.

"But there is one more thing that I need you to warn your friends about," Alciel stated.

The mist changed once again. It formed a towering demon with scales of dismal shadow. Large demon horns reached out from the top of his head. Even as a mirage, Phil could feel his eyes pierce through him. A disgusting yellow eye gazed upon him from his chest.

"I'm sure you remember this demon from the battle with Chaos?" the voice inquired.

"Judgement," Phil said plainly.

He remembered him all too well. He was absolutely terrifying in the battle that Alciel was referring to. As he saw Judgement in front of him, he felt his knees practically buckling beneath him. It was almost too much to bear.

"Judgement will block the path to your friends quite soon. They will have to trust Derek to do the right thing."

"Trust that asshole?"

"That's right."

"Why?"

"Your fate may be tied to the Chaos Gate," Alciel replied. "But Derek's fate is tied to Judgement."

"But I won't be able to do a damn thing," Phil said, knowing that it was the truth.

"Sadly, no, my friend. You will already be dead. I need you to tell Derek of Judgement's arrival. He will know what needs to be done. And you will trust him."

"Well he's certainly never steered me wrong before," Phil sighed.

The mist changed for one final time. Alciel's human form was in front of him now. He painfully smiled at him.

He knew the sadness that gripped Phil. He felt something similar, but he had burdens of his own to carry.

"I'm out of time, Phil," Alciel said. "Don't forget to warn your friends of what is coming. Especially Judgement. Soon you will awaken. You have no idea just how helpful it will be to warn your friends of everything that is about to transpire. You may very well save the universe itself."

The mist and the castle hall vanished from Phil's sight. Then he returned to his body after that trip into the ethereal plane. His eyes sprang open, and he sat right up. He looked around and saw that the others were still sleeping soundly.

"Saving the universe doesn't sound so bad," he whispered.

# CHAPTER 9

# REFLECTION OF A NIGHTMARE

Phil realized that even though he had been so cold, now he was covered in sweat. He had no idea what Alciel had put him through but knew it was unnatural. Normally, he wouldn't be afraid of anything, but seeing Judgement again reminded him of just how terrifying the demon was. The demon holds a magic that could easily turn his friends against him in a fleeting moment. That was something he didn't wish to see happen again.

Roy sat up groggily and tried to wipe the drowsiness off his face. He noticed Phil sitting next to him on his sleeping bag, covered in sweat. He was rather perplexed by his current state.

"You alright, Phil?" he asked.

Phil became aware that he had been breathing heavily, almost as if he was out of breath. Seeing Judgement in that dreamscape must have rattled him more than he had thought.

"Once everyone is awake, we have a lot to talk about," Phil said seriously.

"Alright," Roy said, still half asleep.

The two of them sat there patiently waiting for the others to awaken. It had surprised Roy that the others slept so much. He had expected them to be early risers as soldiers for a secret organization, but that wasn't true at all. They had waited for at least a couple of hours before everyone else finally awoke. Derek was the last of them to wake up. But it was most important for him to know everything. It sounded as if his efforts would be the most important.

"What's going on?" Derek asked sleepily.

"This is gonna sound crazy," Phil replied.

"Crazy is our specialty," he said. "But do go on."

"Well, I had a dream last night, and in it a man warned me of what was coming. It doesn't look good for us."

He got the response that he had expected from Derek. "You woke us up for a man in your dreams?"

"Shut up, Derek," Dedalia ordered.

Derek shrugged but let Phil continue.

"Who was this man?" she asked.

"Called himself Alciel," Phil explained. "He showed me the forms of some terrible creatures. I still don't understand it myself."

"I never would have imagined that it would come to this so quickly," she said, sounding distressed. "Only the prince would have been able to pull something like this off."

"He did mention being some sort of prince."

"Alciel is the Prince of Demons. I'm sure he mentioned it at some point while he was talking to you. He's been trying to help humanity in secret for a long time."

"Can we trust him?" Roy asked.

"More than we can, the king. Barbatos is our greatest threat. Once he is out of the way, then the Immortals are all but guaranteed to fall."

"So, Barbatos is our ultimate enemy," he said.

This king was at the end of his vengeance. He just knew it. Once the king is dead, everything should be over.

"Alciel mentioned that he had wanted to warn us about the Turka as well," Phil continued. "But he wasn't able to reach any of us."

"Makes sense," Dedalia said. "He would only be able to reach us in our dreams. There is no good alternative."

"Am I the only one who thinks that all of this sounds fucking insane?!" Derek shouted in disbelief.

"Stay quiet," Dedalia replied. "The adults are talking."

He rolled his eyes and fell back onto the matted floor of the tent. Then he stared up at the ceiling. This place really was something else.

"What kind of monsters did he show you?" she asked Phil.

"He told me of the Dragizar. They will be the first to arrive. He even said one in particular had a linked fate with Roy."

"What now?" Roy asked. "I don't even know what the hell a Dragizar is, much less how to kill one."

"You'll know when the time comes," she said. "For now, we should warn these soldiers about the impending attack."

"I don't know if they'll have enough time to prepare," Vince said. "The Dragizar are nasty bastards."

"We will have to try."

"Just one more thing," Phil said. "There was one thing that Alciel wanted to make sure that I mentioned."

"What is it?" Dedalia asked.

"The Demon, Judgement."

Derek sat right up. He seemed to go pale after hearing the demon's name. For once, Derek seemed to be fearful.

"You've gotta be kidding me," he said, sounding a little scared. "Anything but that son of a bitch."

Even Dedalia's face seemed to grow pale, and Vince put his head into his hands. He released a loudly dramatic sigh.

"Are we scared of Judgement?" Roy asked, surprised.

"Very much so," Vince said, lifting his head out of his hands. "But for now, we need to warn the soldiers about the Dragizar that are coming. Just rip off one Band-Aid at a time."

Phil knew that he should have mentioned the Chaos Gate to them. But he didn't think they would handle his impending sacrifice very well. For now, he would keep it to himself, and he would deal with it when they reached that point.

"Is Judgement really that powerful?" Roy asked in awe.

He had never seen these people so terrified. The most shocking was Dedalia. Dedalia didn't seem like the kind of person who would get scared easily.

"He is the very same person who tore through our ranks during the battle with Chaos," Vince said, recalling the moment vividly. "He did it all by himself, and it almost cost us everything. Now get dressed. We have a lot of work to do."

"We do?" Roy asked.

"We do. Most of it is in convincing this leader to get up off his ass."

Dedalia had left the tent so she could get dressed without their prying eyes on her. She knew well the lustful hunger of the typical man. The others got dressed in the tent, and they joined Dedalia outside. They made their way towards the Leader's tent, knowing full well that he was probably drinking himself into a stupor. They were greeted by the same two soldiers who were in the front of the tent yesterday.

"The Leader made it quite clear that he doesn't want to see any of you," the soldier on the right declared. "Now turn around and get your asses out of here."

"That doesn't matter anymore," Phil said, ignoring his hostility. "Things have changed. We have come to warn him of the monsters that are on the way as we waste time here talking to you."

"They sound pretty serious," the soldier on the left said, sounding nervous. He glanced over at the other soldier.

"Shut up, man," the first soldier replied. "He doesn't want anyone to go inside right now."

"But what if they're right? I don't wanna die, man."

The first soldier did a classic facepalm with his right hand.

"You're hopeless," he said. "You know that, right?"

"Fuck this," Vince growled. "We don't have time for this."

He walked through the two of them, pushing them aside with his strong frame. The others followed after him. The soldiers were too stunned to stop them. They hadn't expected them to just go for it. The nervous soldier had been knocked onto the muddy ground as Vince's body plowed into him.

Roy looked down at the soldier that Vince had knocked onto the ground. "Sorry about that." Then he continued into the tent with the others.

They burst into the tent to see that the Leader had upgraded his flask. He was drinking straight from the bottle instead. He scowled as he looked upon them entering his tent.

"I know I said no interruptions," he snarled.

The tent was filled with soldiers. At least six were standing nearby, ready with their fingers on the triggers of their guns.

"Sorry, sir," the soldier closest to them said. "We'll take care of them."

"I'm sorry, are we interrupting your freaking Zen time?" Derek asked. "Must be nice to have soldiers wait on you hand and foot while you sit peacefully on your ass."

"Fuck off!" the Leader shot back. "You have no idea the shit that I've seen!"

His words were beginning to slur as he took a swig from the bottle in his hand.

"You're pathetic," Derek said. "These people look up to you. You're supposed to lead them. You're a fucking disgrace of a person."

The Leader drunkenly rose to his feet in response. Then he pointed a shaky hand at Derek.

"Who are you to lecture me?" he asked drunkenly.

"Derek, we don't have time to waste on this idiot," Phil scolded.

He couldn't believe that this man was looked up to by the soldiers here. Still, he was the one they would have to warn about the Dragizar that were coming. He wasn't sure if they would make it through the night in this circumstance.

"You're right, Phil," Derek said. "Things might be different if we did."

"Don't have time for what?" the Leader slurred.

"Monsters are coming. We don't know when, but that's why we're still here. Unless you think your ragtag team of soldiers is enough to deal with them."

The Leader shrugged, unconcerned. "We'll be fine."

"No, you won't," Vince stated. "These are some of the worst monsters there are, and you're in no condition to fight."

The drunken man appeared to be offended. He placed his free hand on his chest, and his mouth dropped open in shock.

"It seems suspicious that you know so much about them," he said, sounding slightly sober already. It was rather impressive. "How can I know you didn't just bring them here yourselves?"

"I don't think there's any reasoning with this guy," Roy said.

"Finally!" the Leader exclaimed. "Someone gets it!"

Just like that, his sobriety was gone.

"Dragizar are coming," Vince said. "They are not to be treated lightly."

"Dragizar?" he asked. "Is that supposed to mean something to me?"

"You don't know about the Dragizar?"

"The only things we've encountered on this glorious shithole have been those damned Immortals."

Vince understood now. These soldiers had never encountered any of the monsters. Somehow the monsters had been contained and just released recently. They wouldn't know anything about the Dragizar, Turka, or anything else this planet had to offer.

"So, what is a Dragizar?" he asked.

Shrieks pierced the air outside the tent, followed by several loud thuds as heavy feet slammed into the ground. More screams echoed from outside as soldiers were slaughtered.

"**Those** are Dragizar," Vince declared. "It sounds like there is a lot more than just one."

"I'm sure that we can handle 'em," the Leader said with a drunken chuckle.

# Chapter 10

# The Dragizar

As Roy and the others conversed with the Leader, a sea of colors streaked through the sky. These are the Dragizar that Phil had tried to warn them about. A total of ten Dragizar raced towards the campsite, each one being a different color.

The entrance of the campsite had a rotted gate closed tight. This was the defense that the soldiers had put into place to repel intruders. The barrier wrapped around the entirety of the camp. Watchtowers loomed over it at each corner of the campground. At each tower's summit, a soldier stood guard. They scanned the horizon in front of them, not knowing what was coming for them.

A soldier situated at the front right tower didn't even see them coming. The thick clouds gave the Dragizar an almost perfect cover. The squad of flying Dragizar veered away from each other and made their move. A Dragizar of sea blue scales soared towards the unsuspecting soldier. The Dragizar held a long spear in its hand as it flapped towards the soldier.

There was a loud whistling noise as he launched his spear through the air. The soldier cried out as the spear pierced his chest, and he tumbled back out of the tower. One of the spokes burst through his chest as he fell onto the fence below. His bloodied body was suspended limply over the fence.

The blue Dragizar took a deep breath, and his human body radiated in a red glow. Then he opened his mouth wide and shot a fireball into the tower. There was a large explosion as the tower was torn apart. What was left of it crashed through the fence next to it.

The destruction caught the attention of the soldier at the top of the left tower. He turned towards the burning tower and saw it was nothing more than a pile of rubble. He saw the blue Dragizar pulling his spear out of the dead soldier's body.

"What the hell is that?" he asked, feeling fear grip him.

In the corner of his eye, he saw the glint of a sword. He whipped himself toward it with his machine gun in hand, knowing that something powerful was holding it. He also knew that whatever it was had the ability to fly. He hated the fact that he was right. A yellow Dragizar was hovering in the air in front of him. It was holding the sword he had noticed a second ago.

He fired his gun at the monster in front of him. The bullets were piercing his human torso. The soldier hadn't realized this was his best move to make. He was more scared and just shooting erratically. In a desperate act, the yellow Dragizar lunged at him and thrust his sword through his chest. The Dragizar weakly crashed through the tower, and a broken, jagged piece of wood stabbed through the Dragizar's chest. He crashed onto the ground with the remains of the tower, lying in a dead heap on the muddy ground.

Screams echoed in the air as the soldiers were killed one after the other. The Dragizar had made their presence known and were unrelenting. Each Dragizar had a different weapon and found varied ways to kill the soldiers. On top of that, the Dragizar burned any soldier that they came across in a fierce blaze. Just to ensure that they wouldn't be able to survive. Then they burned the tents that they passed as well, giving the soldiers no real place to turn to.

The soldiers stood no chance against their onslaught. Several Dragizar were killed as well. But every time that one was beaten, the soldier in question was killed by another one in quick succession. Nothing more than a cruel and vicious circle. A black Dragizar ignored the soldiers and made his way to the Leader's tent, knowing that's where the man in charge would be hiding. The blue Dragizar reached the tent where Derek had his wounds treated and razed it to the ground with the spit of a vicious fireball.

The black Dragizar landed in front of the two soldiers guarding the entrance to the tent. The two soldiers glanced up at the Dragizar, knowing that he was the real deal. He was different from the other Dragizar that were storming the campsite. The muscle on his bald, human torso was just ridiculous. Unlike the others, he was wearing a thick, sinister-looking chest plate over his torso. He was holding a large axe in his right hand and snarling at the two of them.

"You ain't getting inside," the soldier on the left whimpered.

The Dragizar's body glowed in a red hue before he unleashed a fireball from his mouth. An explosion threw the soldier off his feet, and he was sprawled out on the ground next to the tent.

"Who the hell are you?" the soldier on the right asked.

The Dragizar could sense the soldier's fearlessness. At least he had proper courage. But it would soon be put to the test.

"You can call me Drakenith," he growled. "If you are lucky enough to live."

He lunged at the soldier in a flash. He lopped off the soldier's head in a fluid strike. The headless body fell to the ground, and his blood splashed against Drakenith's chest.

"Another worthless creature put in its place," Drakenith said.

He rushed into the tent and saw the scene unfolding. Roy and his friends were in a heated argument with a drunk holding a bottle in his hand.

"So, I've finally found you," he growled. "This is where you die, Roy Darsetts!"

He whirled his axe through the air, and everyone jumped out of the way. The axe narrowly missed Roy and slammed into the Leader's chest. Everyone just stared at the Leader in shock. He coughed up blood all over himself, but then he smiled.

"It's about damn time," he said, smiling.

Then he fell backwards onto the mat of the tent with the axe protruding from his chest. Still, they just stared at him. Derek was the first to snap out of their trance.

"What are you waiting for!" he snapped at them. "Shoot the son of a bitch!"

Everyone was brought back to their senses and brought their individual guns to their hands. Then they shot at the dark menace in front of them. But he was already in the air above them, making it harder for them to hit him. Then he spun down to them. The stream of bullets missed him almost completely as he expertly spun past them. He gripped the handle of his axe sticking out of the Leader's chest and yanked it free. Then he flew back above them.

"Humans!" he declared. "My fight isn't with you. I am here for Roy Darsetts alone. Stand down and allow me his head. Only then will I spare you! If you would stand in my way, I will take **your** heads instead! Make your choice!"

"He tried to warn us of your coming!" a soldier shouted. "We will fight with him!"

"Yeah!" the soldiers yelled in agreement. "Today is the day you die, monster!"

Drakenith smiled at them. "So be it. You have made your choice then."

He dove at the nearest soldier and slammed him onto the floor with a brutal swing of his axe. The other soldiers turned towards him with their fingers nervously on their triggers. This monster had killed their friend in an instant, without any hesitation. There was no remorse in his action. They were starting to doubt their ability to fight a monster like the one before them.

The Dragizar lifted his head, and his stare struck fear into them all at once. But then his torso emanated a piercing red glow. They knew what was coming next, but they weren't sure if they would have enough time to escape it. Drakenith spit a blistering fireball into one of the soldiers. The blast launched him off his feet, and the rest of the soldiers were thrown aside.

One of the soldiers had managed to barely hold his ground. He lifted his gun toward the monster's overwhelming presence. He couldn't help but whimper under Drakenith's gaze. Drakenith rushed at him and hacked off his arm. Drakenith grabbed the wounded soldier by the jacket and lifted him into the air. The soldier felt his body tremble slightly on its own. Then he saw a faint, red glow dulled further by Drakenith's armor. He knew that he was done for.

Drakenith opened his mouth wide and breathed an intense stream of flames into the soldier's face. As the flame engulfed his body, the soldier shrieked in agony. Then Drakenith dropped him onto the damp floor of the tent, his burning body extinguished.

The other soldiers tried to fire at the abomination over their heads, but their aim seemed pathetic compared to the impressive aerial acrobatics that the Dragizar showed. Drakenith skillfully evaded their bullets, seemingly anticipating their attacks. The soldiers were scared. It showed visibly on their faces. Their lack of confidence led to their poor aim. They couldn't seem to focus on the Dragizar. All they knew was that they had to kill this thing before it killed **them**.

Roy's group fired at the monster from the other side of the tent, but it seemed to do little good. Drakenith was in his element in the air over their heads. The whole situation seemed rather one-sided; the Dragizar then decided to make his move.

He soared towards them and maneuvered around their seemingly endless stream of bullets. Then he swatted one of the soldiers aside with a mighty strike of his axe. Drakenith flew back above them before they had the chance to adjust their trajectory, and he spit a blazing fireball into the soldier lying helplessly against the tent's wall.

The explosion devoured the soldier, and the flames stretched along the wall of the tent. The soldier screamed in anguish as the fire enveloped him. This encounter looked rather grim for all parties involved. The remaining soldiers were starting to feel the ever-rising pressure. The increasing flames were reaching for them as they shot at the Dragizar.

Drakenith smiled at the cowering soldiers. "It looks as if the heat is getting to you. Are you not the elite soldiers of the Secret Society? To me, you seem no more reliable than a pair of wriggling worms."

The soldiers' faces twisted into anger. Drakenith knew he was getting to them. Now they were sure to get emotional and rush at him with no regard for their feeble lives. He noticed that their fearful faces were gone. A strong determination took its place.

"Fuck this," one of the soldiers said, reaching into his pocket.

He had pulled out a grenade from his pocket and ripped off the pin. Then he hurled it in the direction of Drakenith. The Dragizar's smile did not fade. Instead, he caught the grenade and balled his hand around it as it exploded. The explosion was condensed into his hand and seemed pathetic to witness. Not a scratch had appeared on the Dragizar's balled-up fist. The soldier's previous determination was eviscerated as he processed what had just happened. His fear had come crawling back to his face. He was trembling as he looked up at the monster in its sinister armor.

"A desperate attempt," Drakenith said, talking down to the soldier in a mocking manner. "However, you failed to consider that I am not a weak creature such as yourself. I have the power of a fucking **dragon**! Fire only makes me stronger! You have doomed only yourself!"

Drakenith whipped the husk of the grenade into the man's face. It bounced off his face after a loud smack, and he tripped into the sea of flames behind him. He screamed in agony as the flames wrapped around him in a hot embrace.

The last soldier felt the incoming flames licking at the back of his boots, but he dared not turn his back on the Dragizar. Roy's group had been firing at the Dragizar the entire time that all of this had been happening. Drakenith was quite good at tormenting his foes while dodging their best attacks. He had made it seem like an effortless art.

Suddenly, a plank ablaze fell from the ceiling of the tent. It fell in the vicinity of Roy's group, forcing them to scatter. This was the moment that Drakenith had decided to strike. He landed heavily onto the ground in front of the final soldier and beheaded him in a swift, precise strike. The headless soldier fell back into the blistering flames. Then he soared back above everyone's heads.

"Damn it!" Roy shouted. "We couldn't save a single fucking person!"

"Just remember that all of this was your choice, Roy Darsetts!" Drakenith shouted gleefully.

"What choice?!" Roy shouted. "You just wanted to kill them for sport!"

"Hmm," the monster chuckled. "You aren't as dumb as I took you for. Too bad it doesn't mean a thing."

"Stop being a coward and come down here to face us!"

Drakenith laughed at the notion. "Me? A coward? Will you still talk tough as I take the lives of your friends as well?"

"We will die alongside our cherished friends!" Derek yelled. "And we will make damn sure that you die with us!"

"I will be more than happy to give you what you want," the monster declared.

He positioned his axe in hand and got ready to dive towards them. Phil knew that this was the moment that Alciel had told him of. He just wasn't sure what he was supposed to do.

"Roy, shoot the son of a bitch!" he commanded.

To his surprise, Roy did exactly that. He was surprised at how successful he was. Roy shot a bullet up at Drakenith, and it sank into the Dragizar's right eye. Drakenith hollered in pain. It seemed he hadn't been expecting it either. He covered his eye with his free hand as the blood streamed down his face. Everyone else aimed their weapons at him. Seeing the dire situation he had put himself in, he realized he had no chance.

"A lucky shot," he growled. "Next time we meet, I, the mighty Drakenith, will take your eye as my own. It'd be best to make yourself stronger for that moment, or you won't be so lucky as you were on this day."

Then Drakenith expertly glided out of the tent. Roy lifted his pistol up toward the fleeing monster. Vince placed his hand on Roy's gun, stopping him from taking the shot.

"Should we be letting him get away?" Roy asked.

He lowered his pistol and placed it back into its holster. He wasn't sure if it was the best move.

"It's fine," Vince said. "You're still alive. That's what matters. Just focus on that for now."

"But won't he want revenge?" he asked.

"He definitely will, but that's not important right now. By the time he finds you again, you will be stronger. I **guarantee** it."

"You just asserted dominance over a powerful monster," Derek said. "Enjoy that. Now that the bastard is out of the way, we are free to continue towards the Commander."

"That's one way to put it," Dedalia said. "But we do need to keep going before something even worse shows up."

"The monster was nothing more than a puppet," Roy said. "We need to keep moving so we can kill the son of a bitch behind all of this."

He tightened his hand into a fist. "He will pay for everything he has put me through."

"Hold onto that fighting spirit, Roy," Derek said, smiling. "You're gonna fucking need it."

Roy knew that the General was responsible for Lyn's death, but still he couldn't help but feel unrelenting anger towards the man who had sent him. He still didn't even know what the man looked like. However, he would gladly end his life for good.

Stepping out of the death-ridden tent, they couldn't believe what they saw. All the soldiers were dead. Not one of them was spared. The tents were all ablaze. Still, all the Dragizar were slain as well. At the very least, the soldiers fought valiantly until their final moments. Corpses riddled the ground everywhere they looked. The Dragizar were as gruesome as their reputation foretold.

"I can't believe it," Vince gasped. "They're all dead. The last of the soldiers who fought alongside us in the service of the Secret Society."

Derek glared over at him. Michael hadn't wanted Roy to know about the Secret Society.

"You know that we're not supposed to talk about the Secret Society, Vince," Derek scowled.

"Right," Vince apologized. "Sorry, Roy. I promised Michael that I wouldn't tell you about it."

"What a bother," Roy replied, disappointed.

Vince guided them through the campsite to the other side, where they would continue their trek through the wasteland that Khais had so graciously offered them. The flames stretched towards them, but they stuck to the moist and muddy ground. This gave them some sort of comfort. Not much of one, but still a small comfort that lingered. The flames were a reminder of just how dangerous and cruel this planet could be.

# CHAPTER 11

# CHAOS GATE

They walked down the muddy trail through the wasteland, and Roy still wouldn't let the Secret Society rest.

"I want to know about this Secret Society," he said. "And why do you refuse to tell me about it. We have a long walk ahead of us. Why not pass the time?"

Derek hung his head in defeat and let out a sigh. "What a pain in the ass. Go ahead, Vince. Tell him about it. It's kinda your fault that he is so curious."

"I suppose we don't have a choice," he agreed. "The Secret Society was a group of soldiers that fought against the supernatural forces that the typical human was blissfully unaware of. We purposefully kept them in the dark about it so they could go about their normal lives."

The rain was starting to pick up again. The rain had kindly provided them with a break while they fought against the Dragizar at the camp, but now it was pouring on them again.

"So why wasn't I allowed to know about it?" Roy asked. "Sounds like they did great things to make the world a better place."

"Michael had wanted to keep your life as innocent as possible," Derek replied. "He didn't want you to experience the darkness that had been trailing behind him. But now it seems that his efforts were pointless. You have embraced the darkness and are walking the same path that he did."

"He chose this," Dedalia said. "If fortune favors us, perhaps he will be the one to subdue the Immortals at last."

"I'd like to share your optimism," Derek said, doubtfully. "But somehow I don't think it will be that easy."

He glanced over at Roy and could see the offense stained on his face. No matter what, he always believed in being bluntly honest. If someone didn't like it, then oh well.

"I'm still rooting for you," he continued. "But the Immortals we have been facing are pitiful compared to the ones coming for us next."

"I feel the encouragement," Roy said sarcastically.

"I'm just giving you the honest truth. Something that these pussies won't give ya. Just remember me as someone who will always give you cold, hard facts."

Roy was ready to continue their conversation, but then Derek stopped. Roy halted his walk next to Derek, and he followed Derek's finger as it pointed to a strange structure in front of them.

"What the hell is that?" Derek asked.

Phil recognized it from his dream as soon as his eyes locked onto it. This is when he knew that his time was soon to come to a sudden end.

"I have no idea," Dedalia said, baffled. "I'm pretty sure that it wasn't there last time that I came through here."

"It's in our way," Vince said. "We will either have to go around it or break the damn thing."

This structure was the gate from Phil's dream. He already needed to tell his friends about it. He hadn't thought that they would reach it so quickly. Somehow, looking at it, Phil knew that Alciel was right. Something about it told him so. He would have to sacrifice himself for his friends to continue. The others wouldn't like what would happen next.

As they got closer, they were able to see just how massive the gate was. It was wedged in between two towering mountain walls. Going around it seemed to be well out of the question. They could probably try to climb over it, but based on its appearance, it could prove to be quite dangerous.

The gate was an ominous black with grooves jutting out from its center into the face of a demon. Red gems were placed in its eye sockets, giving it an eerie gleam. On its right side is a strange platform one step high.

Derek stretched his hand and was able to barely reach the top of it.

"Alright, guys," he said confidently. "We're gonna jump over this damned thing."

A spike sprung through his hand, and he cried out. Then he fell back onto the muddy ground. The blood gushed out of his hand into the puddle next to him.

"Motherfucker!" he screamed in pain.

The spike sprang back into place just as quickly as it had emerged.

"What the fuck is with this thing?"

Dedalia grabbed the bottom of her shirt and ripped off the lower part. This showed off her toned stomach.

Roy couldn't help but be impressed. She went over to Derek's helpless form and bent down. She could see the pain causing tears to well up in his eyes.

"Give me your hand," she said.

"Am I not in enough pain already?"

She gripped his hand roughly, and he howled in pain. Then she wrapped the scrap of her shirt around his hand tightly to stop the bleeding.

"Stop being a little bitch," she warned. "It's not a good look for you."

He rolled his eyes but sat up. His hand was already starting to feel better. But he knew he was going to have a hard time using his weapons going forward. He cursed his own luck.

"You will go nowhere until the price is paid," a booming voice declared.

"Who's there?" Derek asked, grunting as he rose to his feet.

"I am the Chaos Gate. There is only one way through me."

"And what would that be?" Roy asked.

He felt that he was not going to like the answer, but Phil was pretty sure he knew what it was going to be.

"Sacrifice," the voice said plainly.

There it was. What Phil had been so afraid of all this time. He was aware of the harsh reality awaiting him. He stepped towards the gate with his heart feeling heavy. He always made it look like he didn't care, but no one in the group could care more. Alciel was right in his dreams. All of them were his dear friends, and he cherished each and every one of them. Derek pushed him aside roughly.

"Get the fuck back, man," Derek warned him. "If anyone is doing the sacrifice play right now, it will be me. I'm broken enough as is. In both my mind and body. I'll just slow everyone down."

"I didn't think you were the type," Dedalia remarked.

"No," Phil said. "This is my time."

She was actually a bit relieved. She didn't know if she would be able to see him die in front of her.

"What makes you think that throwing your life away instead of mine will change a damn thing?!" Derek asked angrily.

"Based on how real my dream has already become, everyone will need you in the fight against Judgement," he replied. "You are the one to beat, Judgement. Not me. But **you**."

His eyes had welled up with tears. He didn't want to go, but at the same time, he knew that he had no choice. For once, Derek was at a loss as to what to say.

"Who knows what would happen if you aren't there to save everyone?" Phil inquired. "But seeing how Roy was able to stop the Dragizar. I know that everything I saw in that dream is very real. Maybe fate knows what needs to happen, and we are just its steppingstones."

"You're putting too much faith in some dude from your dream!" Derek shouted in frustration. "Fuck that guy, man! You know I can do this!"

"I'm very well aware of the fact you can do this. You are stronger than any of us. Even Dedalia realizes that. This has been hard on me too. But I know that fate has chosen me over anyone else."

"Fuck fate, man! Just listen to me for once in your damn life!"

"It's been fun, guys," Phil said, smiling at them, ignoring Derek altogether. "I loved every damn minute of it. But it looks like my time is at its end."

"Don't do this!" Derek screamed. "No one would miss me but people like you!"

"You're wrong about that," Phil said, glancing over at Dedalia.

"What?" she asked, surprised.

"Her?" Derek asked skeptically. "We hate each other. Isn't it obvious?"

"You aren't fooling me," he chuckled nervously. "I see the way you two look at each other. Just stop denying it and accept it. You two would be great for each other, and both of you know it."

"Now I know you're being delusional," Derek said.

Dedalia shot him a scary look. Derek managed to catch a glimpse of it.

"Clearly, I'm kidding."

She just glared at him with the intensity of the sun.

"Have you chosen your sacrifice?" the voice interjected.

"Yeah," Phil said, his voice cracking, stepping towards the gate.

"You may proceed to the pedestal."

"Stop this shit!" Derek shouted.

Phil kept going toward the pedestal that lay in wait for him. Derek's hands tightened into fists so tight his skin paled to a white. Everyone tried to look away, but Phil kept getting closer to the platform.

"Are we even gonna **try** to stop him?!" Derek asked in anguish.

He knew that his frustration would fall on deaf ears. They had accepted his decision. He refused to do the same. He should be the one up there. Phil was a good person who didn't deserve such a cruel end. Then Phil stepped onto the pedestal. He turned towards them with a smile on his face, but tears were running down his face. He was scared, as he should have been.

"You guys make sure to give those bastards hell," he said. "Make sure they will **never** forget what we have done."

"You talk too much," Derek said, putting his face into his hands, still in clear denial.

Metal, spider-like legs sprang out from the gate and wrapped around Phil's body. He was jerked against the wall of the gate. Still, he smiled at them. Suddenly, eight spikes burst through his upper body. The spikes held him in place as he spat blood all over himself. Then the gate rumbled loudly as it spun him around to the other side.

His blood traveled along the grooves of the gate, giving it the appearance of crying. Then the gate slid open, ushering them forward. The others fought back their tears as they passed through the gate.

"We appreciate your donation," the Chaos Gate said, sounding rather satisfied.

Vince was the last one to pass through. He turned back to face the gate. He took a good look at Phil's mangled corpse and then back at the gate itself.

"If you weren't so goddamn indestructible, I would have torn you apart, piece by piece," Vince growled.

"Then I am lucky that I am indestructible," the Gate replied, unfazed.

"You have no fucking idea," Vince shot back.

Then he followed the others down the trail. He couldn't believe how close they were already. There it was, waiting for them. The Chaos Mansion. The place the Commander would be making his last stand, whether he was aware of it or not. The time had come to make him pay for all the pain he had caused. For Phil's sake and for so many others who had died due to his actions.

# CHAPTER 12

# CHAOS MANSION

The mansion in front of them seemed to get bigger the closer that they got to it. They felt the heaviness in their hearts as they approached it. The death of Phil still lingered among them. Despite their grief, they knew who was waiting for them beyond those doors. The man who was the root of their suffering. The Commander. And now it was time for them to take the fight to him.

The four of them reached a rusty iron fence and were given a harsh reminder of Phil's fate behind them. Vince kicked the front of the gate, and its doors swung open awkwardly. The memory of the Chaos Gate was still fresh in his mind, making him feel rather bitter towards the gate in front of him. The gate stopped at the edge of the path leading up to the mansion in front of them. They proceeded towards their destination, prepared to cause unfathomable pain to the man within.

The ground that they walked through was littered with decay. A cracked fountain was to their right, sadly spitting up water from a battered statue. It was unclear how it was still working, but it stood strong. The trees were dead and crooked, doing everything they could to stand. Rubble of varying size was scattered across their way.

Vince stopped at the front door. He breathed a heavy sigh.

"Everyone ready?" he asked, turning towards them. "It's been a long time, but we finally reached the man we have been searching so long for."

"Just open the damn doors," Derek demanded.

"Right," he said, turning back towards the doors.

Vince kicked them open, and everyone followed him inside the mansion. They looked up to see a balcony, with a curved staircase on either side of it. What really drew their attention was the man leaning against the railing of the balcony in its center. Something about it made them feel as if it would be difficult to reach him.

"The Commander, I presume?" Roy asked, staring up at him with fire blazing in his eyes.

"The very same," the man replied.

He felt nervous seeing the heroes in front of him but kept his cool demeanor at the surface. He knew that they had killed his cohorts. He still couldn't wrap his head around that fact but would need to be careful.

"Are you proud of all the lives you took?!" Roy asked him with a snarl on his face.

"You wouldn't understand."

"No? Because of you, I have no wife to return home to! We all lost a friend just down that fucking trail! But you have no guilt for any of it!"

"This is what I hate about you and your kind," the Commander said disdainfully. "You're all so narrow-minded. You don't try to see the big picture. All you ever focus on is yourselves."

"That's not an answer, asshat!" Derek snapped back.

"I didn't have a choice," he replied. "But consider everything that you have done. Are you really so much different?"

"What are you talking about?" Roy asked.

"How many have you killed in your little quest of vengeance?"

"That's different. You're obviously evil. We are doing the world a favor by taking you out. The universe even."

"Just who the fuck do you think you are to decide that?"

The Commander was growing increasingly angry, and he knew it showed as his voice began to rise. Roy was considering what he had just told him. He certainly had a good point. Derek could see him thinking it over.

"Don't fall for his bullshit, Roy," Derek said. "He's merely trying to save his own skin."

"Only you would see through the message hidden among my words," the Commander said, sounding rather disappointed. "But it won't matter in the end, as you will never reach me. It is time for you to witness the darkness of this place."

He snapped his fingers, and the floor beneath Roy slid apart. They all fell through the hole that appeared beneath their feet.

"No one survives the reckoning of Judgement," he grimaced.

Everyone had crashed onto the hard floor below. It was just enough to knock Roy unconscious but not enough of a fall for him to break anything. When he came to, he saw Vince was sitting next to him.

"Oh good, you're awake," Vince said. "We were waiting for you to wake up before proceeding."

"What happened?" Roy asked woozily.

"It would seem that we fell for the Commander's trap," Dedalia said. "I hadn't anticipated him thinking quite so far ahead."

Roy groaned as he got on his feet and looked around him. Vince rose to his feet next to him. The Commander was right. It was definitely dark down here. He didn't like the look of it.

"I heard him say something about Judgement as we fell," Roy said. "Now I know Phil had tried to warn us about him. So, I'm curious. Who exactly is Judgement?"

Derek sighed with a heavy heart. "If he's really down here, then we are in deep shit."

"Judgement is one of the ancient demons," Dedalia explained. "One of the most powerful demons in the king's ranks. He possesses a rather peculiar magic that will be difficult to deal with if he truly is down here."

"I'm sure he's here," Derek said worriedly. "I feel like I can sense him. The second you see him, you need to shoot the son of a bitch. Or we are all fucked."

"Sounds like you have some history with him," Roy observed.

"I've seen firsthand just how potent his damn magic is. He turns good people into his freaking puppets.

"We'll just have to be careful then," Vince said.

"I only hope that will be enough," Derek replied.

They fumbled their way through the large, dark room. It proved to be more challenging than any of them had expected. Eventually they reached a stairway that led out of the room. The light from upstairs was peering down into the room they were in, giving them a good look at their new adversary.

A tall, slender demon stood in their path. If he stepped out of the light, it would be impossible for him to be seen. His skin matched the darkness of the room. He had a large axe propped on his shoulders. His red eyes gleamed excitedly upon seeing them. He seemed particularly excited to see Dedalia among them.

"Welcome, heroes, to my domain," he said excitedly.

# CHAPTER 13

# ANCIENT DEMON, JUDGEMENT

"I must admit it has been quite lonely in this abysmal place," the demon said.

"You're lucky I didn't kill you the last time that we met," Derek growled.

"Still, you worry your little head over that?" the demon asked.

"You killed my father, you piece of shit. Right in front of me, even."

The demon let out a chortled chuckle. "The look on your face made it all worthwhile. Like the one you have now. But the best part is, I would do it all again."

Derek glared up at the demon unflinchingly.

"What the fuck do you want?" he asked the demon.

"It's not what I want," Judgement said. "It is what **he** wants."

"The Commander, right?" Derek said, shaking his head in disbelief. "I didn't think you would listen to anyone but yourself."

"When it benefits me," he said. "I am willing to help others."

"I should have known."

"You see, the Commander wants all of you dead. **Him** especially."

He had pointed in the direction of Roy. "He seems to be scared of you the most. Not sure why. The ones I wanted to play with the most would be Derek and that bitch in your group. Now, shall I turn the two of you against each other or against everyone else? Or everyone else against you? Decisions, decisions."

Derek's face got serious instantaneously. "No matter what happens. Do not look that son of a bitch in the eye, got it?"

He looked around at the others. They seemed confused. They realized that he knew something that they didn't. It was unnerving.

"So, you know my secret, do you?" the demon questioned.

"What do you even mean, Derek?" Roy asked.

"Just trust me!" Derek shouted. "Don't look in his fucking eye!"

"Having a lover's quarrel, are we?" The demon chuckled.

"You can stay the fuck out of it!"

He looked at the others grimly. For once he was more serious than he had ever been. He wasn't sure if he would survive this moment. But he would make sure the others made it through this. He was beginning to understand what Phil meant before he died. He had to be here for this fight. He was the only one who **could**.

"Just promise me," Derek said, looking around at the others.

"We got your back," Vince said.

"I've never seen you so serious," Dedalia said, surprised.

"Nothing has ever **been** more serious," Derek said, turning back towards the demon.

Judgement slammed his axe onto the floor next to him. It stood propped up on the ground next to him. Then he held his arms out wide in an inviting manner.

"Stare deep into my all-seeing eye, children of humanity!" he declared. "Allow me to show you the way to be free of pain and suffering!"

The eye on his chest flicked open and radiated a bright yellow. Derek knew the others would have a hard time not staring into it. He was having a difficult time himself. He lifted his arm to better cover his eyes.

"Don't resist, Derek," Judgement said. "It will only break your mind ever further."

"Shit, shit, shit!"

With his arm still covering his eyes, Derek drew his pistol and fired. The bullet pierced the demonic eye on Judgement's chest. Blood gushed down the demon's body as he squealed in pain.

Judgement staggered back into the wall behind him. He was in disbelief as to what had just happened. Derek had shot out the source of his power with a lucky blind shot from his gun. The demon pushed himself off the wall with anger on his face. Derek lowered his arm, curious if he had been successful. The fury on Judgement's face brought the realization that he had eradicated Judgement's magic. The demon hoisted his axe into his arms. Then, in a quick motion, he slashed Derek's head off his body. It had been almost as clean as if Drakenith had done it.

Roy and Vince were in shock as Derek's head rolled on past them. His blood sprayed from his headless body, and it crumpled onto the floor. It was like a bad dream. Derek was dead. They heard a springing noise, and Dedalia ran past them with her spear at the ready.

She thrust the pointed blade of the spear through Judgement's right shoulder. He winced in pain as more of his blood trickled down his arm.

"You bastard!" she screamed in an ear-piercing rage.

Judgement gripped the handle of the spear and lifted her up so that the two of them could see face-to-face.

"Did you feel something for that pathetic man?" he asked.

"I felt **everything** for him!"

"A pity."

He flung her off the spear, and she smashed against a wall. The wall seemed to tremble before she fell to the floor. Without even turning to face her, he threw the spear back at her. The pointed end stuck to the wall next to her face.

"As much as I wish to have fun with you," he said. "Your friends are keeping me quite busy. I will deal with you momentarily."

Both Vince and Roy had their weapons sprung out and ready. Their eyes were stitched into a fiery determination. Judgement shifted his shoulders, and the sound of cracking echoed loudly.

"I do admire your courage, mortals. But it is foolish. Challenge me, and I can assure you, you will share the fate of your dead friend."

"A demon wouldn't understand," Roy said.

"Then you're welcome to throw your lives away. Maybe you will be better than him, but more likely, you will fall as well. The outcome means nothing to me. Both of you will still die.

He lifted his large axe into his arms. Roy and Vince ran at him without hesitation. The axe swung down toward them, and Vince met it with his own. Roy slipped under the axes and sliced the demon's side. Judgement kicked at Roy's legs, and Roy stumbled sideways. He fumbled but managed to regain his balance.

Vince was struggling to hold his axe up against Judgement's strength. His feet began sliding backwards across the floor. Roy stabbed the demon in the back, and his blade appeared near his shoulder, where Dedalia had stabbed him.

"Begone," Judgement said, clearly annoyed.

He jabbed his elbow into Roy's unsuspecting face, and Roy was flung backwards. He slammed against a wall and slipped down onto the floor. His nose felt broken from the force, and blood was running down his face. Vince ducked under Judgement's axe while he was distracted. Then he swung his axe into the demon's chest, causing him to stumble back.

Dedalia had regained consciousness and blinked the scene into focus. She was impressed by how well Roy and Vince were taking on such a powerful demon, but she felt that they could use a hand. She stood up and pulled her spear out of the wall. Then she ran towards Judgement, screaming with her spear pointed in his direction. She thrust the pointed end at the demon's face.

A black wisp had blocked her advance. It was not what she had expected. A bald man in thick, dark armor had appeared. He had grasped the spear's tip between two fingers. His eyes were blazing red as he looked down at her.

"Who the hell are you?" she asked, fuming.

He saw the fire in her eyes and felt no concern. His expression being cold and empty.

"Trust me, girl," he said. "You are far from being able to challenge me. You've done enough. I have plans for this worthless creature."

"Get the hell out of my way!" she demanded. "I will kill the bastard!"

"It seems I wasn't clear. You will not so much as scratch me."

"Move, and I won't have to!"

"Maybe I should have introduced myself after all. I'm the Chaosbringer, all of the darkness in Chaos' soul given form."

"So, what if you are?"

The Chaosbringer sighed. "Why are the mortals always so dense? Except you aren't one of them, are you? Just a fake, trying to fit in."

He snatched the spear out of her hand in a fluid movement and hurled the blunt end of it into her chest. She was whipped backwards through the air and pinned to a wall. The spear held her high enough for her feet to dangle in the air. She spat black blood all over her body. If the spear had been facing the other way, she would have been dead. He didn't wish for her death. He only wanted to show her just how out of her league she truly was. As she hung from the wall by her own spear impaling her, she came to a grim realization. This man is on another level entirely.

Roy couldn't believe what he had just witnessed. Whoever this guy was, he had just made short work of the strongest among them. The Chaosbringer turned toward him.

"Roy, you have no idea how lucky you are," he said. "I will not kill you today. It would get in the way of my plans for what is to come. But do not be mistaken. It would be such a simple task for one such as I. Fate has all sorts of fun plans in store for you. Before your journey reaches an end, you will die. It just won't be by me."

Roy just stared at him blankly. He had no idea what to say. That was quite a lot to take in with so few words. He would die. It made him wonder if there was even a point to any of this.

"It seems I broke him," the Chaosbringer said, turning towards the others. "I'll let you all deal with that. But I will be taking this imbecile with me."

He placed a hand on Judgement's shoulder, and the two of them vanished in a puff of darkness. Roy and Vince turned towards Dedalia with a look of shock. They never would have imagined Dedalia could have been beaten so easily. She stared at the two of them, looking increasingly annoyed. It looked rather strange with the tip of her spear protruding from her chest.

"Are you two jackasses gonna get me down or what?!" she barked.

# CHAPTER 14

# DEAL OF A DEITY

Judgement looked around at his new surroundings, knowing this was a place much worse than that basement in the Commander's mansion. He recognized it as the Void. He had hoped to avoid this place for at least another couple of centuries. He was on a platform over the Void's still nothingness. Broken pillars tried to reach upwards from the ground. All the while, rubble swirled about in the air around the platform.

The Chaosbringer stood in front of him, patiently waiting for him to come to grips with his situation. Judgement honestly had no idea why he was worth saving in the first place.

"Why did you bring me here?" Judgement asked.

"I have plans for you," the Chaosbringer replied. "I can't have you dying just yet."

"You let Parallax, Alioth, and even Servisus meet their end," he said. "Why am I so important?"

"I would have you fight alongside more worthy demons. Ones who may even match your strength. But I also know that you will do exactly what I expect from you."

"And what would that be?" he asked.

"I think you know of these demons quite well, Judgement. You should be pleased to get the chance to fight with them as your allies once again."

"What are you even talking about?"

"I will release the four elemental demons. In the off chance that they are beaten, you will destroy Roy once and for all."

"So, I'm nothing more than a last resort?" Judgement asked, feeling his blood boil.

He gripped the handle of his axe tightly as it lay on his shoulders. The Chaosbringer could see that he wished to strike him down.

"I wouldn't do that," the Chaosbringer warned. "You know I would kill you before it even reached me."

"You could, but I know that you won't."

"It seems that you are actually aware of how important you are to my schemes," he replied. "Before I am able to free your allies, however, I need to get Lazeras to make his move. Once he falls as well, then even Barbatos will realize the urgency to release them."

"What about Baelor?" Judgement asked.

"Here I was thinking you had figured it out. No. Baelor is already dead. He just doesn't know it yet. We must plan for his inevitable downfall."

"What do you mean?"

"Baelor has foolishly pushed the mortals too far. He has given them the reason that they need to fight. This makes them dangerous to all of us, but more so for him. He was the one who set the motive right at their feet. His actions led to the death of Roy's wife, and now he wishes to kill Baelor more than anyone else. He is focused solely on him. This allows us to continue our own fight from the shadows while they are busy dealing with him."

"You're psychotic," Judgement said. "Why won't you just intervene and kill them all?"

"I have bigger things to worry about than them."

"What could possibly be more important?"

"I have much more scheming to do," the Chaosbringer said. "I will even let our king fall as my plan permits."

"Are you out of your damn mind?" Judgement asked in disbelief.

Judgement didn't want to believe it. This man was plotting the death of their king. And worse yet, he seemed to know everything that was about to happen. He was just letting his fellow demons succumb to their horrific deaths rather than helping them. Judgement felt that he was worse than even the most hated of demons.

"Everything I'm doing is for a singular purpose," the Chaosbringer said, noticing Judgement's dismay.

"What fucking purpose?!"

"To reunite with my other half," he said with a slight smile on his face.

"What?"

"All of this is to bring the Lightbringer forth. This is the best way to get his attention. Once we are reunited again, we will become Chaos once again in his complete form."

"Who the hell is this Lightbringer?" Judgement asked quizzically.

He had never even heard such a name in all his long life. He had heard many names in his lifetime. But that one had never graced his ears.

"The Lightbringer is all the goodness contained within Chaos' soul. Both of us are required to merge the soul once again. Once we are one, then the soul will be one again. Then, we will assume the shape of Chaos, the demon of complete darkness, and swiftly conquer Earth.

"If you're so damn powerful, then why the hell do you even need me?" Judgement asked.

"I don't," the Chaosbringer replied. "But fate says that you are necessary at a certain point in time. Fate has taken me a long way, and I won't be denying it now. It has been very good to me."

Judgement tightened his grip on the axe he held. "And what if I refuse your maniacal plans?" he asked.

The Chaosbringer laughed loudly but then saw the seriousness on Judgement's face.

"Seriously?" the Chaosbringer asked. "You know who I am and what I can do to you, right?"

Judgement was unflinching. He didn't like any of this. He certainly didn't want to help the man in front of him.

"Perhaps you need a reminder," the Chaosbringer said, his face twisting into a hideous snarl.

The Chaosbringer stretched out his right hand to the air in front of him. A funnel of darkness began twisting in front of his hand into a long shape. The shadow had turned into a large sword that he had gripped from the air. An aged skull was placed in the center of its hilt, while glowing red runes trailed down the blade. The edges of the blade seemed to be jagged teeth.

Judgement was intimidated by the new demeanor that the Chaosbringer had shown. The Chaosbringer jabbed the demonic blade through Judgement's uninjured shoulder. The demon screamed in pain, and the Chaosbringer quickly ripped the blade free of his shoulder. Judgement fell to his knees, and the Chaosbringer looked down upon him. Judgement could see the look of a disdainful god gazing down at him. Even as a fragment of a deity, he was vastly intimidating. Fresh blood began running down Judgement's shoulder.

"Remember this moment," the Chaosbringer told him. "If you ever think of refusing me, I will tear your miserable body apart and scatter it across the fucking Void!"

Judgement pressed a hand to his new injury in hopes of, at the very least, slowing the bleeding, and he looked up at the Chaosbringer. Fear was etched on his face. He should have expected this. He began to notice just how eerily similar the Chaosbringer was to Chaos himself.

"Defy me again, Judgement, and I will not be nearly as lenient," the Chaosbringer promised.

He disappeared in a cloud of darkness. Judgement slowly rose to his feet and saw another demon approach him. She was an elderly demon. He recognized her immediately. She was the Dark Messiah, the Seer Demon, once the right hand of Chaos. Now imprisoned in the depths of the Void.

"Are you his newest plaything?" she asked.

"So, this is where he sent you?" Judgement asked, sneering down at her.

"I allowed them to bring me here," she replied.

He looked at her, quite perplexed. "Why would you want to be in a place like this?"

"This is where I am meant to be."

"Nice place," Judgement said, looking over his surroundings.

"I know how it seems," she said. "But this place isn't so bad."

"No? Then why is this place chosen as a punishment?"

"It all depends on how you look at it."

"And how is it you look at a place like this?"

"It is a tranquil place that allows me to expand my mind."

Judgement couldn't stand looking at her and turned his back to her.

"I know why you were brought here," she said.

"Do you now?"

"Would it change anything if I told you that the Chaosbringer's days are numbered?"

He whipped back around to face her. "You jest. Have you seen that son of a bitch? He's untouchable!"

She cackled. "Difficult, maybe. But not untouchable."

"What are you scheming?"

"The only way to outthink a schemer is to think three steps ahead of them."

"And how is it that you accomplished that?" he asked.

"He came to me for a prophecy," she said. "I gave him one, but one of the most important details was false."

"What do you mean?" he asked, gripping the handle of his axe.

"The prophecy has nothing to do with our king or even Chaos himself."

"What?!" he asked, getting frustrated.

He pulled the axe off his back and into his arms.

"The prophecy is about an even greater being. One who is called Lucifer. He is far more powerful than either of them."

"So, you lied to the Chaosbringer," he said quietly but angrily. "Not only that, you put my king in danger for no reason."

"You know my reason," she replied nonchalantly.

Judgement lifted his axe into the air. "Then I have no choice but to end your treasonous existence!"

He swung his axe onto the top of her head; a mess of blood splattered around her. He grunted as he freed his axe from her skull.

"This is… how it… was… supposed to… be," she said before falling onto her back in a dead heap on the ground.

"Fuck!" Judgement shouted in fury. "I'll have to find a way to explain this to that crazy son of a bitch!"

# CHAPTER 15

# FRIEND OF A LEGEND

Back on Earth, a large man wandered through the streets of New York. He would be a powerful ally to Roy moving forward. However, Roy was completely unaware of his existence. Much less everything that he had been trying to do for them. He had made a promise to Michael that he had every intention of keeping. He would do everything in his power to make sure Roy lived, no matter what. He knew about Roy's unfortunate situation with the supernatural. Now he just needed to support him from afar and keep him alive.

He stood six feet tall with short, spiked hair atop his head. He has an eye patch draped over his right eye with a claw-shaped scar stretching across it. The tight shirt barely contained his bulging muscles. His jeans were fading denim and had definitely seen better days. He was once a dear friend to Michael Darsetts. He is Jake Slayon, a demon hunter so skilled he is only second to Michael himself.

Jake stepped into a bar and embraced the clinking of glasses as he entered. He got a lot of stares, but he was used to it at this point. His appearance was not easy for many people to accept. He sat down at the counter. The bartender glanced at him nervously and made his way over to him.

"What do you need?" the bartender asked him.

"Beer," Jake said. "Something strong."

"You got it."

The man began assembling his drink from behind the counter. Jake couldn't help but wonder how he had gotten to this point. He had attempted to keep tabs on Roy, but it hasn't gone well. His tracking tech had failed him during the cusp of Roy's greatest struggles. This is why he had spent most of his days drinking. It could get even worse if he fails Michael, too. He just didn't know how he would be able to live with himself if he did. The bartender finished his drink and slid it over to him.

"Enjoy."

Jake simply clutched the glass in his hand and tried to clear out his mind. Push the negative thoughts out and focus on finding Roy. He could feel in his gut that Roy wasn't dead. He just knew it. He had let Roy do his own thing for quite some time. Not knowing where he was made him feel like he was failing him all the same. Maybe things would be different if he could just find him. He trusted the people that Roy had become fast friends with. This was a small comfort at the very least.

He took a deep swig of his drink and felt the bitter flavors rush through him all at once. This is how he planned to access the deepest recesses of his mind. He didn't know if he would have any better luck, but it couldn't hurt to try. He took another gulp of the mind-numbing alcohol and let it course through his system.

He wanted to know how far they had come, but at the same time he was nervous about what he would find. He pulled out his phone and smacked it roughly on the table. This could very well be his last chance. If he still couldn't find them, he might as well just call it quits. He would be of no help to them anyway. But then the news report on the TV caught his eye.

The report detailed the deaths of multiple men recently due to various accidents. Just by glancing at the television, he could tell these accidents were setups. Something far worse had happened to them that the public wouldn't be ready for. It seemed that the Secret Society still had a strong influence over the media. For that he couldn't be more grateful. He shot back the rest of his drink. He tapped the counter to get the bartender's attention.

"Same thing?" he asked.

"Yeah," Jake said dryly.

The bartender began making him another drink. The images on the screen were rather blurry for him, but he knew that he recognized those faces. He had been part of the Secret Society with Michael for a long time. He saw those faces plastered all over the place. In fact, he knew all the Immortals and what they looked like. Just one of the many secrets that he had kept.

The bartender slid him a new drink, and he grabbed it in his hand. He squinted at the screen and saw a mugshot of Elliot. He was sure of it. He took a sip from his drink. To him, though, Elliot went by another alias. The Worker. An Immortal who was notorious for disguising himself among office workers. He would kill his target when they least expected it.

"Damn," Jake said, impressed. "He's actually doing it."

"What?" the bartender asked.

Jake hadn't realized he had spoken out loud. The bartender was probably confused.

"Oh, I knew the guy who was on the TV," he said.

"The guy's a freaking psychopath," the bartender said, seemingly to scold the man who had been on the TV. "He brought a gun into the middle of someone's wedding."

"No kidding," Jake said, sending more alcohol down his throat.

Then the screen changed and showed the image of the Sergeant. The bartender saw the man's face appear on the screen.

"That man destroyed damn near half the city," he said, shaking his head in disapproval. "What is this world coming to?"

"Hand me the bottle," Jake said, ignoring the bartender's inquiries.

The bartender unscrewed the top and slid him the bottle. "I don't know why any of this even matters. These men were nothing more than deadbeats who only lived to make others suffer."

"You may be on to something there," Jake said, taking a chug from the bottle.

He savored the flavor flowing down his throat. None of the other Immortals he had been searching for had appeared on the screen before the report ended. He took another swig before looking back down at his phone.

Things were finally starting to make sense. Maybe soon, he will be able to find them at last. Somehow Roy and his friends had managed to kill Elliot and the

Sergeant too. Based on the information on his phone, the Lieutenant is dead as well. His phone didn't say by whom, but he had figured that Roy's group had a hand in that too. They had come a lot further than he had ever thought possible. But having the Secret Society's database on his phone sure had its uses.

He shot back more beer down his throat and glanced down at the tiny, slightly blurred screen in front of him. There was a new update. The General is dead. He nearly spit out his beer in surprise. Roy had actually done it. He bested the man who had put him on this path in the first place. He couldn't have been prouder of him. But he couldn't even fathom all the different thoughts surely swimming around in his head. At this point, Roy could probably stop right now. There would be no more need for senseless killing. But he felt that he wouldn't. His anger with the Immortals would likely only get worse over time. He would have to be there and guide him through it.

He scrolled through the database and saw some disheartening news. Both Phil and Derek were now dead as well. He needed to find the remnants of Roy's group soon. Their lives may depend on it. He didn't want to see any more of their deaths appearing on the tiny screen in front of him. He knew that they would be going after the Commander next. He was the one who sent the motivation to them in the first place. But as their numbers fell, so did their chances of being able to win this.

"Fuck," he breathed.

"Are you good?" the bartender asked, concerned.

"No," Jake replied dryly. "Far from it."

He slapped a hundred-dollar bill on the table. "For your trouble. Keep the change."

Then he drained the rest of the bottle down his throat and slid it back to the bartender. He rose from his chair groggily and stumbled out of the bar. He needed to reach the old headquarters of the Secret Society. It was his only real last chance to be able to help Roy and the others. He was running out of time. Even with all of the luck Roy currently possessed, he didn't think the three of them would be able to defeat Baelor. His overwhelming power would overtake their emotional weakness. They wouldn't stand a chance. They wouldn't be in their right mind in their battle against their greatest foe yet.

Everything around began getting distorted. He was buzzed as he made his way down the sidewalk, but he knew exactly where he needed to go. He had been there more times than he could count. Soon he would join the fight and make the Immortals sorry for the day they had messed with the Darsetts family.

# Chapter 16

# Jake Slayon

Jake knew that he looked like a drunken mess as he wobbled down the sidewalk. He didn't have time to worry about it. His phone chirped to inform him of a new notification. He roughly pulled it out of his pocket and clicked the notification on his screen. It showed a blurry red dot on his phone. Roy and his group had reached the Commander's mansion. He was honestly impressed. He wasn't so sure if Roy would be able to get as far as he had. Still, he needed to hurry. It was only a matter of time until they reached the Commander himself. He would need to be ready for that moment once it came.

He shoved his phone back into his pocket. He would be able to put the new information to good use soon enough, but he required something a bit stronger than his phone. He just needed to reach the Secret Society's building. This is where he would have access to everything that he needed. He only hoped that he sobered up enough by the time he made it inside to better use the computers.

As he lumbered his way towards the building, his mind began to wander. It was still quite the walk. He needed a better way to pass the time. He was reminded of the time that he had lost his eye. Although it was not a pleasant memory, it would help him pass the time more quickly as he approached the building he was looking for.

***

It all happened a couple of years ago during the battle with Chaos. He was one of the few who were chosen to go to the planet where Chaos dwelled. It was the planet of demons. This place is known to all as Hell. A planet full of nightmares, where demons were the least of your worries.

He was making his way through molten caves with Michael at his side. But in no time at all they had reached **him**. The one who had taken everything from everyone. Chaos, demon of absolute darkness. He is considered a god in his own right. Definitely not the one you would want to pray to. The kind that would require a sacrifice if you wished to live in his presence.

Chaos is a large demon blanketed by scales in the shade of night. Chaos dwarfs even the largest human in size, his eyes adorned with crimson streaks. His physique was godlike, and the way he carried himself was as if everyone was beneath him. He knew he was better than everyone. Now he was sitting on a throne to match his demonic presence. A large sword was stuck to the ground next to him. The darkened hilt of the blade was molded to a strange shape. It looked as if it had twisted into the visage of a dark creature's face. Not exactly a demonic face, but it embodied something even more sinister. The long, jagged blade itself was a bloody red shade. The color of the blade made it easier to conceal any blood that may stain its surface.

Chaos rose from his seat and sneered down at them. Putting his godly personality on full display. Jake and Michael fought against him with everything that they had. Michael wielded but a single sword. Jake had an axe in one hand and a shield in the other. The shield proved to be useless, as it was knocked aside early on in the encounter. The massive blade was swung towards him, and he managed to jump out of the way.

But it wasn't enough of a leap. The tip of the blade scratched the right side of his face. This was the moment that he lost his right eye. He pressed his hand against the streaming blood that ran down his face. At the time he had no idea how lucky he was. Chaos lifted his blade up in anticipation of finishing him off, and Jake stumbled back. He tripped and fell on his back. He had been taken off guard.

Chaos brought down his blade, and Michael met it with his own. He pushed against Chaos' blade with as much force as he could muster. He knew it wasn't even close to deterring the god in front of him.

"Jake," Michael strained.

Jake struggled to his knees. It proved harder due to keeping one hand on his face. Though at this point it didn't seem to be slowing the bleeding all that much. But he looked at Michael through his blurred vision.

"What is it?" Jake asked weakly.

"I need you to get out of here," he said.

Michael could feel his knees buckling under the demon's strength.

"Why?"

"I can't have you dying here. I need you to find my brother. If I die here, I need you to make sure that he lives. Nothing else matters to me. I don't want him getting wrapped up in all of this supernatural shit. Guide him to a carefree life. Have the Secret Society help you. You know which people would be best for keeping him safe. Just make sure he gets that peaceful life that he deserves."

"I can't just leave you here!"

Michael glanced over his shoulder at the broken man behind him. He knew that he wouldn't be much help in this fight. Still, he couldn't help but admire his tenacity.

"I need you to do whatever it takes to keep my brother safe."

"I can still fight!" Jake shouted in clear denial.

"No, you fucking can't! Promise me!"

Michael's feet slid back on the brimstone floor. He knew he wouldn't be able to hold Chaos back much longer. The demon grinned at him, acknowledging his unavoidable reality.

"Leave me, you stubborn son of a bitch!" Michael screamed.

Jake struggled to retrieve a Portoball from his pocket. He was still hesitant about leaving a good friend behind to fend off such a monster.

"You better make it out of this shit!" Jake demanded.

"Just go, damn it!"

***

That was the last thing that Jake had remembered from Michael's fight with Chaos. He didn't know if Michael would come back alive or dead. What he did know was that he would keep his promise to him no matter what. He would sacrifice himself if necessary. But he would ensure Roy's survival.

Jake stumbled against a chain-link fence, bringing him back to reality. He put his hand over the scar upon his face as he was reminded of the struggles the two of them had faced. It felt as if it could have been just yesterday. Then he dropped his hand back to his side and realized that he had arrived. Just as he knew he would. Even in a daze, he would know his way to this place. The headquarters of the Secret Society.

He made his way over to what looked like a tollbooth. This is where a soldier would verify if someone was be allowed entry to this secret place. If not, they would be turned around without hesitation. Now the booth had no roof, and most of it had been torn apart. The sliding gate was now a twisted mess on the ground. He made his way over the twisted gate and headed towards what appeared to be a rather plain building. The balcony for a second floor looked down on him. The structure of the balcony itself was riddled with several holes. He reached the front door, which had at one point required a constantly changing code to access. The keypad lay broken on the ground, sparking at his feet. It was a sorry state, to say the least. He pushed the pair of front doors, and they collapsed into the building. It was amazing they had stood as long as they did.

"What a mess," he sighed disappointedly. "It's sad to see how far we've fallen."

He stepped inside and heard the crunch as his shoes met with the littered rubble. The inside wasn't much better than the outside. Even in the state of everything, he knew that the computer he was looking for would still be intact. He reached an elevator and pressed the button to bring it to him. By some miracle it still worked. It sounded as if it had a difficult time reaching him, though. He made his way inside and pushed the button to close the doors. Then, at the push of another button, the elevator began its descent into the lower levels of the building.

He went down five floors before the elevator dinged. The doors slid open, and he stepped onto a floor that looked untouched by the destruction above it. He was hoping for it, actually. The technology down here was probably among the most important in the entirety of the facility. He had entered a laboratory that was once manned by a woman who was known to all as Tricia Deathbed. She was a big deal when she worked alongside them. He stopped at the door leading deeper into the lab and looked at the plaque hanging neatly beside it. It simply read *Tricia*. She never did like titles. Not that she could ever have been mistaken for anyone else.

Jake took a deep breath before entering the lab. There was a small chance that the machine he wanted to use might not work. Although the likelihood was slim, it was still a possibility. He passed by several tables piled with science equipment. Brilliant people do have a habit of hoarding things most people would deem unnecessary.

Over the years, Tricia had crafted some particularly useful gadgets for the Secret Society. She had used some of those gadgets on a daily basis. Jake wandered past most of it, not needing it for what he had planned to do. He wouldn't have a clue how to use most of it as is. He reached a computer desk. This is the only desk in the entire room that is not covered by anything. Most of the recordings of information would be here.

Jake sat at the desk and booted up the computer. The computer was requesting a password. He would have to think like her. What would she put in her computer on a daily basis? She was married to Derek's brother, but somehow that seemed too easy.

Maybe it would have something to do with the prophecy that had been going around before Chaos met his end. It mentioned Darsetts, but he wasn't sure if it referred to one of them or both of them. If Chaos was resurrected, it could involve Michael or Roy. He plugged in *Darsetts Two*. The computer granted him access.

Jake chuckled to himself. "Always focused on what matters the most. Never change, Tricia."

He activated the program that he would need, and the image of a Portoball popped up on his screen. He was going to create one of his own and go help Roy's group against the Commander's fury. All he needed to do was program their location into the device. Using his phone as guidance, he began plugging in commands into the computer. He only hoped that he would be able to reach them in time. A lot was riding on how quickly he would be able to do this.

"Give it your all, Roy," he said, feeling the pressure in front of him. "Just hold on, the vanguard is coming."

# Chapter 17

# Deadly Motivation

Back in the Commander's mansion, Dedalia stared at Roy and Vince intensely as she hung from the wall by the handle of her spear. The Chaosbringer had really done quite the number on her. Her body had taken serious abuse, but so had her pride.

Roy and Vince strolled over to her nervously. They gripped the shaft of the spear and tugged on it. Still, she was suspended above them.

"Put your damn backs into it!" she demanded.

"Sorry," Vince apologized.

They tried again until they had managed to pull her free from the wall. She landed on her knees and grabbed the handle of the spear. She jerked the spear out of her chest, and the black blood spilled onto the floor in front of her. She cringed as the wound began closing itself up. She was breathing heavily. Even though that wound wouldn't have killed her, the pain must have been excruciating. She jabbed the handle of the spear into the floor and used it to lift herself onto her feet. The two of them just stared at her in amazement.

"Now, was that so hard?" she asked.

Then, with the push of a button, she retracted the pointed tip of her spear and holstered it on her back. She turned towards Vince, ignoring their shock and awe.

"I can't believe you took a jab at my weight," she said. "Fortunately, right now we have an Immortal to vanquish. Otherwise, I would have made you suffer quite severely."

"My bad," he apologized. "I wasn't thinking."

"Clearly not. We need to find where the Commander is hiding in this place. That is our only priority."

"Do we even stand a chance anymore?" Roy asked. "Two of us have been killed in quick succession. Maybe we got a little overzealous."

Not too long ago, he had been thrilled to wipe out the Immortals one by one. Now he had lost his morale after the loss of not one, but two good friends. Dedalia grabbed him by the face and turned it toward the headless corpse, which was Derek.

"Do you see the remains of that man?!" she asked angrily.

"Y-yes," he stammered.

"Do you know all that he sacrificed for you? Would you just let all of that be for nothing?"

"I-I-I suppose not."

"You suppose?!" Dedalia asked, her fury increasing steadily. "That man was my friend longer than I've known you. Stop wallowing in your self-doubt and stand on your own two feet. That is the only way to beat these bastards. We will beat them, and you will put your best foot forward! I will be damned if I let you die after we've come so far!"

"You're right," Roy said, clenching his hands into fists. "We need to give these guys hell."

"More of us may die, Roy, but it doesn't matter. You were chosen. Not **us**. The Immortals need to be stopped no matter the sacrifices that we make. I mean, we are fighting for Lyn's sake. Are we not?"

She let go of his face, and she smiled as she saw the renewed vigor on it. He turned away and began storming towards the innards of the mansion. He quickly left them behind.

"You're a bad influence," Vince said, rushing after him.

"I don't care," she said, following after him. "I won't let Derek's death be for nothing."

"You really did care about him, didn't you? Why didn't you ever tell him?"

"Couldn't risk overinflating his massive ego."

Vince laughed. "Couldn't be any worse than keeping it as a poor secret."

"Let's just keep moving."

"You know, Michael will be pissed if Roy dies after your little pep talk back there," he said.

"He won't die," she assured him. "Not while I'm here."

"Aren't you the confident one?"

"Just shut up and keep your eyes on him."

"Yes, ma'am."

The three of them searched the rooms one after the other. The rooms seemed to spawn infinitely. They were about to give up hope of ever finding him. But then they found one final room.

They paused for a moment to catch their breath. Then Vince kicked the door open. The trio made their way inside. The Commander was behind his desk, peering out at the muddy wasteland beyond. The rain pattered heavily against the window. It seemed the rain would never end in this place.

The Commander turned towards them rather dramatically.

"Well, well, well," he said. "Look who came crawling back to me."

# CHAPTER 18

# THE COMMANDER

Roy stood in front of Vince and Dedalia with a fiery look in his eyes. His hands clenched into fists. The Commander noticed his burning resolve, but he couldn't afford to let it bother him.

"So, you're the one who sent those assholes after me," Roy said through gritted teeth.

"So, what if I am?" the Commander asked him. "Did you come for any reason other than yourself? You have dragged these poor souls a whole planet away, just so you can have your vengeance. Maybe you will feel better. But in my eyes, it was all a waste of time on their part."

"You don't know anything about me!" he shouted at him furiously.

The Commander chuckled. "I have a reputation to uphold as the Commander, one of the hands of the Demon King. I will be damned if I let down my king! I will strike you down before you even think of pursuing him!"

"Sounds to me like you're nothing more than another pawn."

The Commander's calm demeanor disappeared and was replaced with anger. His eyes narrowed onto him dangerously.

"You dare talk to me in such a manner?! Do you not fear me?!"

"Before all of this started, I may have feared you," Roy replied. "But after all the pain and suffering I have endured over the past couple of years, I have changed. I should fear you. But all I see as I look upon you is an alien that needs to be reminded of what is right and wrong. Because of you, my wife is dead, along with two incredibly good people. I refuse to allow your bloodlust to be satisfied any longer!"

"Do you believe yourself to be strong now?" the Commander asked. "You were given nothing more than a slight glimmer of hope, and now you see yourself as a savior to the universe?"

"You wouldn't understand," he said. "You are an agent of destruction. That **hope** is what has kept me going. No matter how little hope I have, it will be enough to keep pushing me forward."

"Then it seems that I must eviscerate what little hope that you still have left. There is no room in this world for something as trivial as hope!"

"Enough talking! It is time that you return to ash so that I can continue on my path to vengeance!"

He drew a pistol in his hand with such speed that even Derek would have been jealous and shot the Commander directly in the chest. The Commander stumbled back with a surprised look on his face. But then he smiled at him.

"You really think you're walking out of this room alive?" he asked. "Damned fool."

Roy shot him a second time, and the Commander thrust his arms fiercely up into the underside of his desk. The desk spun through the air. Still, Roy fired at his foe, hoping his bullets would pierce him through the desk. No such luck. The bullets simply lodged themselves in the surface of the desk, now spinning through the air. The desk crashed into the three of them. Wood splinters burst into their bodies as the desk slammed into them.

Dedalia grabbed the desk as it collided with them. The trio was knocked against the wall behind them. Roy was knocked unconscious after smashing against the wall. Vince hung onto the desk weakly but was still standing. Dedalia and he exchanged a quick glance and nodded at one another. She hurled what was left of the desk at the Commander. He swatted it aside as if it were nothing more than an irritating fly.

The two of them brought out their weapons, ready to rush their opponent. They would bring the fight to him.

"We will bring this son of a bitch down together," Dedalia declared.

"Let's do it," Vince agreed.

They advanced towards the Commander together, and he laughed at the very notion.

"Truly?" he inquired of them. "Acting as a team has never helped before, has it? Why would you even bother with it now?"

"Shut the hell up!" Vince demanded.

He swung his axe fiercely at the Commander's face. The Commander stepped aside and kicked Vince in the stomach. He was thrown roughly against a wall and collapsed onto the floor. The wall had barely withstood the attack. Dedalia rushed at the Commander and swung her spear like a blade. She had hoped the awkward motion would distract him and give her an opening. He grabbed the handle of her spear with little effort.

"You've always been so brash," he said, unimpressed.

He kicked her in the chest, and she went sprawling backwards. He held her spear in his hand and spun it around, studying the features of her weapon intently. Dedalia shattered the bookshelf that was behind her, and an onslaught of books rained down on her. She fumbled out of the pile of books and felt anxiousness grip her as the Commander seemingly studied her spear.

"So, this flimsy little toy is what you've been using to kill my best men?" he asked. "**This** was supposed to be the tool of my destruction?"

He snapped the spear in half over his knee and tossed the pieces aside. Dedalia felt a sense of dread gripping her. That was one of the best chances she had against this guy. Now it lay on the floor, a broken mess scattered across the room. She tried to hide the fear on her face but knew that it was pointless.

"Whoops. Guess it won't be much help now, will it? Too bad."

Vince put his arm around the Commander's neck from behind in hopes of choking the air out of him. The man's face was changing color, but he didn't seem particularly concerned. Vince knew that he had, at the very least, distracted him. Dedalia ran at him as he flipped Vince over his head. Vince slammed onto the floor and groaned as the pain rushed through his back.

Dedalia let loose a powerful punch to the side of the Commander's face. He stumbled sideways, and she punched him again. He seemed to be dazed as she kicked him in the stomach. He was thrown into a wall, cratering it as he fell to his knees. Vince was now on his feet, standing beside Dedalia.

"Let's kill this son of a bitch," he said, cracking his neck.

"Gladly," she said.

The Commander stood up as they ran towards him. "It won't matter how many times you try; I will put you in your proper place every single time."

Vince ducked under a punch launched by the Commander. He had figured out his movements and was ready for them. He violently swung his axe into his side. The Commander winced in pain and latched a hand around Vince's throat. He lifted him into the air.

"It seems you've gotten far too comfortable," he said. "No matter. I will have to remind you of just how feeble you truly are."

The Commander whipped Vince through the air like a ragdoll. He crashed through the door that had led them all into this room. The door slid down the balcony, still upright, with Vince stuck against it. He smashed through the balcony's wooden railing, and the door clattered to the floor. Vince was sent tumbling through a statue nearby and rolled across the floor. The battered door that lay next to him was the last thing that he saw before he lost consciousness.

Dedalia grabbed the back of the Commander's jacket, knowing it was her last real chance at besting him. Not having her weapon would make this quite difficult. She launched him against the large window overlooking the wasteland. The window didn't break as she was hoping for but cracked instead.

"Shit," she breathed.

"Looks like I need to take you three seriously after all," he said. "I was beginning to wonder how my best men were beaten by such weak humans. Maybe I was wrong about you after all. But now any last shred of hope you have, I will extinguish personally."

There was a gunshot that struck him perfectly in the chest, and he stumbled into the window. Still, it held strong. The window was surprisingly durable. Roy stood next to Dedalia, holding his pistol out in front of him, shaking rather nervously. His nerves were starting to show. This was the man who had set everything into motion. It was a lot to take in. All he knew was that he needed to bring him down no matter what. The Commander seemed to be surprised by his action.

"Well, look who woke up from his nap," he said in a mocking tone. "You're a bit late for the fateful fight, though, kid. Sleeping away while your precious friends fight with everything they have. Now they are all but beaten, and there isn't a damn thing that you can do to me with that little peashooter shaking in your nervous hand."

"Shut the fuck up!" Roy screamed in fury. "You don't know a damn thing about me. You don't know shit about humans. Even when we are at our lowest, we persevere. We survive. We fucking **win**. You are nothing more than another obstacle we will fucking break!"

Roy unloaded his bullets into the Commander all at once. Each bullet pressed the Commander against the window as it sank into him. There was a click as his gun had grown empty.

"Feel better?" the Commander asked rather sarcastically.

"Fuck!" Roy shouted.

He shoved the pistol back into the depths of his jacket and brought out his hilt. He brought out the blade.

"You're the one responsible for Lyn's death!" he shouted. "She was the only light I had in my shit life! You're the reason I'm in this fucking mess! I will kill you so she can finally rest in peace!"

He ran at the Commander with blade in hand, angry tears welling into his eyes. He reached the Commander and swung his blade at him. He was left stunned. The man had caught the blade in his hand. His red blood dripped onto the floor. The Commander knew exactly the danger that this put him in. This vessel wouldn't be able to take much more of this abuse, allowing his true form to come out. He just needed to give these heroes a little push so that he could become free. Roy was in a state of utter disbelief. He relished the look now on Roy's face.

"I don't know where this courage of yours comes from," the Commander said. "But it is pointless, I assure you."

The Commander kicked Roy in the stomach, forcing him to reel forward. Then he grabbed Roy by his jacket and flung him against a wall. The wall nearly crumbled from the force, and he drifted down onto the floor.

***

While the Commander was busy toying with Roy, Dedalia had reached the pointed half of her spear. She picked her spear up off the ground and couldn't believe everything that had brought them to this point. The Commander was now standing over Roy's limp body.

"Now how shall I kill you?" he asked. "Even better, how shall I kill your friends you seem to care so much about?"

He was completely unaware of Dedalia's presence. He felt safe enough, knowing that her weapon was broken much like her spirit.

"Baelor!" she shouted.

The Commander turned his back on Roy and faced her. He looked confused as to how she knew his real name. Only a select few could possibly even know that.

"How?" he asked.

Then she chucked the spear tip into his chest. He winced in pain and felt the blood streaming down his body, and he looked down at the spear tip lodged in his chest, disbelief showing clearly on his face. He just couldn't comprehend it.

"This is for Derek!" she shouted. "You son of a bitch!"

She rushed at him and tackled him through the window. The large window shattered instantaneously, and their bodies were immediately soaked by the pouring rain. There was a large splash as the two of them crashed into the muddy ground. She slid off him to catch her breath. She had thought it was all over. Finally.

But then she glanced over at the beaten Commander and realized that she had forgotten about something important. The Commander had gotten on his knees with the broken spear still sticking out of his chest. He was smiling wickedly at her. She knew exactly why. His skin was turning gray as his body flailed crazily. Of course, the Commander would release his demon before dying.

"You have got to be kidding me," she said exhaustedly.

# CHAPTER 19

# BAELOR

The man who had once served as the Commander was slowly turning into something else even more horrific. His body was twisting into the shape of a gray, grotesque demon. Two curved horns sprouted from the top of his head. Dedalia looked up at the towering entity as it just seemed to keep getting bigger. Scars lined his body, and black spikes began forming all along his body. He stared down at her with eyes to match the Void.

She couldn't believe it. This monster was nearly as big as Parallax was. Still, she was getting the vibe that he was even stronger than he was. He seemed to be an almost perfect fusion of Parallax and Alioth. It was frightening to look at.

"At last," the demon spoke in a booming voice. "You have given me the space to stretch my legs."

Dedalia could feel her hands shaking as she looked up at the behemoth. She knew it wasn't fear but burning fury. Sure, he was intimidating, but she was only reminded of the senseless deaths that he was behind.

"So, you finally showed your ugly face," she said without fear. "Baelor, Barbatos' right-hand abomination."

Baelor absorbed her insults and smiled widely. "You don't need to put on a tough act in front of me. I know that there is fear flowing through you. As one of the two elder demons, I know more than you would think. But I serve Barbatos unflinchingly. His will is **my** will. No matter how determined you are, I cannot allow you to leave this place."

"I am tough," she said, gritting her teeth. "I will break you, you towering freak show."

Baelor chuckled. "I can hear the fear trembling in your voice, girl. You cannot hide it from me."

Dedalia saw her broken spear at his feet and sighed.

"Damn it," she sighed, hanging her head.

Baelor had followed her eyes. She had expected that he would. The spear must have fallen during the Commander's transformation.

"Go ahead," Baelor beckoned. "I will give you a chance. Come for your pitiful weapon. Not that it will do you any good."

Dedalia knew better than anyone not to trust a demon. Especially not one with a stupid grin like the one curled up on Baelor's face. But she knew it was the only chance she had.

"Fuck it," she whispered.

She sprinted towards her broken spear, hoping that she would be able to reach it in time. She wasn't so lucky. The demon swatted at her with his right hand. She pulled the spear out of the ground and thrust it into his hand. He cringed in pain but lifted her into the air as she still held tightly onto the shaft of her spear.

She clung desperately to her broken weapon, now protruding from Baelor's hand. He took his other hand and slapped her off the spear. She felt like she had been hit by a truck, and she went flying in the direction of the Commander's mansion.

She smashed back into the mansion. She broke through a wall and then another until she finally reached the entrance. She smacked onto the floor and slid past Vince, groaning in pain. If not for the wall blocking her way out, she would likely have kept on going. Baelor's sheer strength is just ridiculous.

***

Vince had regained consciousness shortly before Dedalia had tackled the Commander through the window. Shortly after, Dedalia burst through the wall beneath the balcony. She slid right past him on the floor. He wasn't even sure if she was still conscious. He looked at the massive hole in the wall and shook his head.

"This is probably a bad idea," he sighed.

He sprang out the blades of his axe and ran up the stairs leading up into the Commander's office.

***

Roy weakly got to his feet and saw the colossal demon standing outside the window. He walked towards the monster, knowing that it was the last thing between him and his vengeance. He paused at the edge, hearing the broken glass crunch underneath his shoes.

"What the hell are you supposed to be?" Roy asked rather curiously.

"I am the one held in the confines of the Commander's very soul," the demon replied.

"So, you're the ugly bastard who took everything from me!" he shouted, knowing all that he needed to know.

Roy brought out his hilt and pressed a finger onto its center, bringing forth his blade. He pointed the blade at the giant demon in front of him.

"Hmm, chosen ones can be so dramatic," the demon said.

"Chosen one?"

"You weren't even aware of your importance to humanity? How pathetic. Keeping their own savior in the dark. I'll bet you think you can beat me, right? Allow me to save you some time. It doesn't matter how much stronger you got on your little journey; you will never beat me."

"Don't look down at me, demon," Roy said, looking up at him with boldness. "I get that you're powerful. I may not stand a chance against one like you. But still, I will fight with everything that I have and maybe even bring you down with me. Today is the day I avenge my fallen friends!"

"The Immortals will **never** perish," the demon replied dryly. "This is nothing but a minor setback. But to keep more of them safe from your onslaught, I will end you here and now!"

Roy leapt off the window frame, blazing vigor in his heart. He shouted as he soared towards Baelor. The gargantuan demon swatted him aside as if he were nothing. Roy crashed against a cliff wall and dropped onto the muddy ground with a heavy thud.

"Humans," Baelor scowled. "Have always been so brazen."

He turned towards Roy's battered body and stomped towards him. Just in front of him, Baelor halted and raised a large fist to the clouded sky.

"This is where the so-called chosen one meets his end!" he declared. "I will finally get the recognition that I so rightfully deserve from my king!"

He heard more shouting and turned back to his mansion. Vince jumped out of the window with an axe in hand. Surely, he knew that he wouldn't be able to reach him.

"Are you serious?" Baelor asked in disbelief.

But then Vince hurled his axe at him. He had not been expecting this. The axe spun into his chest. The pain had been more than he had anticipated, but not enough to slow him down. Baelor watched as Vince splashed onto the muddy ground in front of him. Vince groaned in pain but was having a hard time getting back on his feet.

"What a disgrace," Baelor remarked. "Waste of my time."

He turned back towards Roy. "Now where was I?"

***

In the headquarters of the Secret Society, Jake was watching Roy's progress from a second monitor. The primary monitor displayed how far along the programming had gone. It was taking longer than he would have liked. It would be cutting it close.

'C'mon, motherfucker!" he shouted at the screen in front of him.

He turned back to the secondary screen and watched as Baelor stood over Roy, ready to deliver the finishing blow.

"Initializing complete," a pleasant voice said. It reminded him of the one that Delkeg had programmed into his car.

He grabbed three other Portoballs from the drawer in front of him. These would be used to help Roy and his friends reach a place where they could finally heal their wounds. But that was a matter for another time. Rather convenient all the same. He shoved the Portoballs into the pockets of his vest. The Portoball in front of him seemed to glow in a luminescent light. He jabbed a finger into the red button in its center.

***

Baelor had brought a powerful fist toward Roy's unguarded body. But something happened that shouldn't have. A large man appeared out of thin air and blocked his punch with a large, rounded metal shield.

"What?" Baelor shouted in surprise.

He pushed his fist against the shield in hopes of knocking this new person aside, but the man wouldn't budge.

"Who the hell are you?!" he growled.

"I'm surprised that you don't remember me," the man said, sounding offended. "We both were in that battle just a few short years ago. But I suppose for an old man like you, that would be a fleeting memory."

Baelor whipped his arm back and shot another punch at him. Once again, he was stopped by the shield.

"What is this madness?!" he screamed in rage.

The man smirked at him. "I'm Jake Slayon, just a humble demon slayer. Surely you can do better than this."

The demon lashed out at his shield in a frenzy.

"I'll be honest," Jake said. "I'm here at the behest of a promise I made to a good friend of mine. Now it's time for me to do what I do best. Slaying demons."

"Why is my power as nothing?" Baelor bellowed in frustration.

"It is quite simple," he explained. "I'm wearing a pair of Pressure Gloves. They were crafted by one of the Secret Society's finest. Tricia, a genius woman, made them, with the sole intent of your demise. She made some of the best weapons to use against your kind. Now these Pressure Gloves give a feeble little human like me supernatural strength to better combat a giant demon like yourself. Not used to the human fighting back, are ya?"

Baelor's punches enhanced themselves into a flurry of anger. Intent on breaking through the shield.

"No human could possibly match our power," he snarled. "No matter the trinket in their possession."

"Go on then," Jake taunted him. "Show me just how tough you are, big guy."

Baelor scoffed at him but then threw his punches more aggressively. The speed and power did nothing against the sturdiness of Jake's shield. Jake remained motionless as the shield absorbed every strike.

"Fuck!" Baelor screamed.

He began panting as he was brought to a state of exhaustion. Jake smiled at him.

"My turn," he said.

He slapped Baelor's hand away with his shield and quickly whipped it up into the demon's face. Baelor felt the air around him go into a haze as he was thrown off the ground. There was a large splash as he slammed onto his back. The shield had rebounded back into Jake's hand.

Baelor got to his knees and screamed in absolute rage. Jake knew that he was pissed. Exactly as he had planned it. He knew that Baelor was a proud demon. Being treated like something so trivial would infuriate him. This made things look good for him.

Baelor rose to his feet and glared down at him.

"I will break your pitiful body, you insignificant whelp!" he shouted.

He rushed at Jake with murderous intent in his eyes. Jake lifted his shield up, ready to face the monster running towards him. Baelor swung a gigantic hand towards him. He grabbed the shield and tossed Jake high into the air. He smiled, as he had anticipated this. As he aligned with the demon's face, he hurled his axe at the monster. It sliced through Baelor's right horn. The broken horn slid to the ground with a heavy splash, while Jake's axe stuck to the cliff wall behind the massive demon.

Jake splashed onto his right knee, making another splash. It hurt more than he liked, but this was all part of his process. He peered through the heavy rain to get a better feel for how far away Baelor was. But then he saw his large hand piercing through the rainfall. He grabbed his shield off the ground and lifted it up to meet the hand. There was a loud clang, and Jake was flung backwards. The shield could only do so much against Baelor's overwhelming power. Jake slammed against a cliff behind him.

"Look at that," Jake groaned. "You're finally hitting like you mean it!"

"Silence!" the demon ordered. "You miserable fool!"

Jake grunted as he stood up and ran towards the cliff face, now harboring his axe. Baelor smacked him into the air, and he was sent spinning against the wall he had been hoping for. The pain was far worse than he had imagined, but he noticed his axe sticking out of the wall next to him. This couldn't have gone any better. He knew that he had figured out Baelor to the letter. Only Baelor was completely oblivious to it. He would use this in his favor.

Jake gripped the handle of his axe and pulled himself up onto his feet. He pried his axe free of the cliff wall and turned towards Baelor. The demon let out an ear-piercing roar in his fiery fury.

"Game's over, Baelor," Jake said.

"Game?" Baelor asked.

"This whole time I was just seeing what you would do," he explained. "Just observing you. Now I know what it is that I need to do to kill you."

"Bullshit. I refuse to perish by the hands of a simple creature such as you."

Jake chuckled. "Your blind faith in your strength is why you have already lost."

Baelor let loose another roar of anger, and Jake chucked his axe through the air. The blades sunk into the demon's face right in between his eyes. He screamed in agony, but he stopped in his tracks as he processed just how much danger he was in.

"This is your end, Baelor," Jake declared.

He whipped the shield into the handle of the axe. The blades sunk deeper into his skull, and he shrieked in pain. It was a rather grotesque, guttural scream. Baelor fell over backwards onto the muddy ground with a wide reaching splatter of the puddles murky water. Jake knew that Baelor was dead before his body even started crumbling to ash.

"The big ones are always so full of themselves," he sighed.

He wandered over to the ash where his weapons had fallen. He reached down to pick them up and strapped them to his back. Then he saw Roy regaining consciousness and headed toward him.

# CHAPTER 20

# THE PROMISE

Roy woke up to the visage of a tall, muscular man wearing an eyepatch walking towards him. He had no idea who he was and instinctively reached for his sword. There was no telling if the man was going to try to finish him off or something worse. He lifted the blade off the ground and pointed it up at him shakily. His body was betraying his sense of mind.

"Who the hell are you?" Roy asked nervously.

He started to notice the flecks of ash floating around in the air as the windy rain pushed them off the large pile behind them.

"Well, I certainly recognize that tone," the man said. "It's just strange hearing it from someone else. I am Jake Slayon. I'm a friend of your brother's."

Roy looked around, not knowing what had happened while he was out. As he noticed all the ash swirling in the air, he couldn't help but wonder if Baelor could be dead.

"Did you kill the bastard?" he asked. "Is Baelor really dead?"

Jake chuckled. "I think the evidence speaks for itself. You've already seen firsthand what it looks like when a demon dies."

"Right," Roy said, feeling dumbfounded.

He had finally done what he had sought out do, but it wasn't by his hand. Now that his new friend had helped him reach his goal, he wasn't so sure what he was supposed to do next.

"Want a hand?" Jake asked, offering his to him.

Roy clasped his hand, and Jake brought him onto his feet. Roy retracted his blade and returned it to its spot on his back.

"Now let's find your friends," he said.

Jake stopped next to Vince, still struggling to get on his feet. Jake helped him up and placed his axe into his arms. Vince holstered his weapon and looked at Jake in disbelief.

"I don't believe it," he said in awe. "How did you even get here?"

"It's a long story," Jake replied. "Good to see you still remember me."

"How could I forget? You were quite the big deal in that battle with Chaos."

"Michael did far more than I ever could," he humbly replied.

"I refuse to believe that. You were the one who helped pave the way for him. Don't let anyone tell you any differently."

"I'm honored, Vince. Just know that very few of us got through those ordeals without any sacrifice. Still, things may have played out quite differently if I had fought alongside you in that battle."

"We may have won without as many losses," Vince replied.

"I don't know about that," Jake replied, pointing out his eyepatch.

"I would consider you to be pretty lucky. If the only thing you lost was an eye during a fight with a literal demon god. It could have been so much worse."

"You have no idea," Jake agreed.

Dedalia was leaning against the hole in the wall leading into the interior of the mansion. She appeared to be in rough shape, but she was still okay. That's a good sign at least.

"Were you planning to leave me here?" she asked.

Roy could tell that she would be just fine. "Of course not. We can't leave behind the muscle."

"You say that as you're being escorted by a couple of lunkheads," she quipped.

"Now that's offensive," Jake stated.

"I've been called worse," Vince replied.

Jake shook his head in disbelief. "Somehow, I'm not surprised."

They reached her, and she looked them up and down. Vince and Roy looked to be in a miserable state, while Jake just looked as if he took a quick shower. Not even a scratch was on him from the struggle.

"Looks like you got your asses kicked pretty good," she noticed.

"Maybe you guys," Jake chuckled.

"Fuck off, man," Vince shot back.

"Still, you guys did a good job keeping the Commander busy for as long as you did," he said seriously. "I barely made it here in time. But thanks to all of you, no one else had to die unnecessarily."

"Is that right?" Roy asked.

"If you hadn't fought him off as long as you did, all of you would probably be dead right now."

"What about her?" Roy asked, gesturing at Dedalia.

"I still could have died," she replied honestly. "If Baelor had gotten his hands on my weapon, he could have easily brought me to a gruesome end. He easily had the upper hand against even me."

"That's kind of a scary thought," he said.

"Regardless, Jake. Why are you **really** here? I know that you won't be sticking around. Even though it would make all of this so much simpler."

"Why not?" Vince asked, turning towards Jake, sounding rather disappointed.

"With one elder demon down, I will need to track the other one as quickly as I can," Jake explained. "I must go to the Secret Society's headquarters and find all that I can about the other elder demon. He is even more powerful than Baelor in his own right. He is named Lazeras. Some of you know of him already, but I doubt Roy would have heard the name."

Roy looked at him quizzically, but the others knew quite well of Lazeras. It was written all over their faces.

"Lazeras," Dedalia said.

She knew the demon well. A woman named Tricia had talked about him without end during their time in the Secret Society. Knowing what he would be capable of, she knew things were about to get much worse. Exactly what she was afraid of.

"I haven't heard of anyone like that," Roy said.

He looked around at the two other nervous faces and knew that they did. Just more secrets that they had kept from him. He was sure he wasn't going to like what they would tell him. This Lazeras must be quite dangerous.

"I figured as much," Jake replied. "Once I find him, I will come once again to help you in your fight. Until then, just promise me no more of you will get yourselves killed."

"As long as they stick with me, they should be fine, Jake," Dedalia said. "But I can't guarantee anything for sure."

"That will have to be good enough," he sighed.

He pulled three Portoballs from the pockets of his vest and handed them to each of them.

"For now, I want you three to use these Portoballs to get yourselves patched up. I know that Dedalia will be fine, but rather safe than sorry, right?"

"I know this place you're sending us to," Dedalia said.

"Of course you do, Dedalia," Jake replied. "You're returning to Earth."

"You know that's not what I mean," she said.

"My brother wanted you to do all this for us?" Roy asked.

Jake clapped a rough hand on his shoulder. "That's right. I promised him I would keep you safe from the supernatural threat that strikes from the shadows. Even when you think that you are alone, I will support you from afar."

It was a comforting thought, but he couldn't help but wonder how much Michael had really done without his knowledge. He had kept so much from him. He was rather anxious about what else he could have kept hidden from him.

"Now, though, I need all of you to press your buttons and get out of here," Jake said.

"Right," Roy said.

All of these lies over the years. Roy had thought that Michael had been a businessman, but he was something very different. He had been hunting monsters for his benefit. The whole time Roy had been none the wiser. He had no idea about the struggles that Michael had endured. He was beginning to see his brother in an entirely different light.

He pressed the button on the Portoball clutched in his hand, and the others did the same. Jake had stayed behind in a place that he had deemed to be dangerous. So, he couldn't help but wonder why he hadn't asked for their help. Maybe he really didn't need it. Jake was quite strong all on his own. He felt that he had been worrying for nothing.

Khais was left behind them, and a piercing white light intruded into his eyes. He recognized the layout of a hospital, complete with the white floors, walls, and ceiling. They stood in a hallway that stretched ahead of them in a tube of brilliant porcelain.

"Where are we?" Roy asked, squinting past the reflecting whiteness in front of him.

Roy glanced over at Dedalia and saw that she was supporting him on one arm and Vince on the other. Jake had been right after all. She didn't really need this place, but he knew that he wasn't in good shape himself. Vince appeared to be a battered mess.

"It's a hospital, obviously," Dedalia replied bluntly.

"I can see that," Roy shot back. "But how?"

"This is where the Portoballs were meant to take us," she explained. "The two of you could definitely use the time to recover. You both look like shit."

They reached a lobby bleached in white. Even the desk, chairs, and tables were bathed in the shimmering whiteness.

"It just seems strange that they would take us to a random hospital on Earth," Roy replied, perplexed.

"I'd rather not give away the surprise," she replied.

"Surprise?"

She stopped in front of the desk, and Roy fell against it. The pain from all his newly obtained wounds began rushing through him. He looked up to see a pretty woman behind the desk. She was adorned with floral pink scrubs, and her brunette hair was bound into a bun.

"Jesus, Roy," Dedalia said, grabbing the back of his jacket.

She pulled him up off the desk and back on his feet.

"I know you're hurting," she said. "But you need to get your shit together."

"Dedalia," the woman in scrubs said.

"Hey. These two could use some treatment. They had a bit of a rough time with some nasty supernatural creatures."

"Got it," the woman said pleasantly. "I'll be sure to let Drakia know."

She wandered through a door behind the desk and escaped through the brightness of the room.

"Who's Drakia?" Roy asked.

"You really ask too many questions," Dedalia replied, sighing.

"Naturally, because I have no idea what is going on anymore," he said. "The bastard who put me on this path is dead. What other reason is there for me to not just go home and take a nap?"

"You poor fool," she said.

"What?"

"You're the one who wanted to eradicate the Immortals. You said so yourself. Considering that, this is just the beginning. So, you better buckle up for the ride."

"Barbatos is the one we want, right? The demon king?"

"At least you're catching on. You still got a lot to learn, Roy. Not to worry, though, Drakia will explain the purpose of this place."

"You're not trying to get rid of me, right? Have this doctor take me away?"

"Wouldn't dream of it," she said. "I have every intention of honoring my promise to your brother."

She was starting to look annoyed. He was starting to feel woozy. He wasn't sure if it was from all the wounds he had endured or something else entirely. But then he saw her. The woman that they were waiting for. She has long, black hair. The doctor's coat seemed to flow around her and accentuate her curves. She was gorgeous. The doctor approaching them now is Drakia.

"Drakia?" Roy asked, mesmerized.

"That would be me," Drakia said, smiling at him.

The nurse with the pink scrubs returned to the other side of the desk, and Drakia turned towards her.

"He's not on any drugs, is he?" Drakia asked her.

"None that we are aware of," the woman replied with a smirk.

Roy looked aghast at their exchange. Did he seem like he was on drugs? Maybe he was worse off than he had thought.

"Just a joke," Drakia said, laughing. "Gotta lighten this tension a little bit. You guys all look so serious. I already know why you're here."

"Then you know more than I do," Roy replied.

"Don't worry," she said. "You'll be glad that you came to me. Just follow me."

She turned her back to them and began making her way down the bright hallway.

"Don't have to tell me twice," Roy muttered.

His eyes unconsciously lingered over her butt for a moment, and Dedalia cleared her throat loudly. His eyes shot back up.

"I will drop you," Dedalia whispered in his ear.

He gulped and focused his sight on the back of Drakia's head instead.

"What was that?" Drakia asked ahead of them.

"Nothing," Roy whimpered.

"That's what I thought," Dedalia whispered.

The three of them were brought into a vacant room. Roy and Vince were each put into their own beds. Dedalia settled into a chair nearby. However, she seemed to be keeping a sharp eye on the two of them. Roy especially. Once Roy had laid back onto the bed, Drakia began going to work.

"As I'm sure you might have guessed by now," Drakia said. "We are not a normal hospital by any means."

"You don't say," Roy replied.

"If you hadn't suffered any injury by a supernatural creature, you would not be able to find this place," she explained. "It would be completely invisible to you. We excel in healing wounds that a normal hospital simply wouldn't be able to handle. So, just relax, Roy. The pain will only linger for a little while longer."

She stuck her syringe into a vein popping out of his arm. He felt pain instantly and winced as it flared up his arm. But in mere seconds, the pain had dulled. The wound on his arm, from one of the many times he had been thrown around like a rag doll, began to fade into nothing.

"Are you sure this is medicine?" he asked. "**Not** witchcraft?"

"I assure you it's not witchcraft," she chuckled.

# Chapter 21

# King's Visit

Far from the Commander's mansion lies a sinister castle of darkness. It is perched atop a cliffside over a lake of lava. Inside is a man wandering its halls with a hood pulled over his face. He made his way through several twists and turns before finally reaching the throne room. He pushed open the overly large doors and waltzed inside.

Barbatos sat on his throne, seemingly relaxed. As he saw the hooded man enter the room, his expression changed. A large demon blade stood at the ready next to him. He would use it only when necessary. He put his face into his hand and sighed but then looked back up at the man approaching him.

"Why are you here, Sorcerer?" he asked, a twinge of disappointment in his voice.

The man slicked back his hood, and his long dark hair trailed down his back. A small goatee lingered beneath his lips. With a snap of his fingers, a staff materialized from the air. It was a brooding dark color with a skull placed at its tip. Purple gems were gleaming in the eye sockets. He was smiling at Barbatos as he snatched the staff out of the air.

"I guess I can't fool you," he said with a grin.

"Get to the fucking point," the king growled. "I don't have the patience for your games."

"As you wish," the Sorcerer said, bowing before him. "I have news about the champion that the Chaosbringer so graciously picked out for you."

Barbatos took a deep breath. He didn't like where this was going.

"What is it?" he asked as calmly as he could.

He had a feeling that in a moment that would change.

"Baelor is dead. As well as his minions."

Barbatos stood up hastily with a blaze in his eyes. His anger had been brought forth. "What?!"

"I'm sure you know what that means," the Sorcerer replied.

"All it means is that I underestimated the mortals," he growled. "Now an elder demon is dead because of it. I must admit I doubted that they would be able to pull it off."

"I would suggest that we find the Maker and convince him to be smarter than Baelor was."

"You make that sound like a simple feat."

"It could be. We will just have to choose our words carefully, and he may very well make them suffer in ways that they never thought possible."

"I will need to see if he's done assembling my army. It may be time for a little visit."

"I think you are right, milord."

Barbatos wandered towards him. He had decided to leave his sword behind. He didn't feel the need to shed any blood today.

"Indeed, I am. Take me to him. We have much to discuss."

The smile on the Sorcerer never changed. "But of course, milord."

The Sorcerer placed a hand on Barbatos' shoulder, and the two of them vanished in a puff of darkness. The Demon King had only wanted to deliver a message. He knew the Maker's ways. He found them to be peculiarly lazy at best. Somehow, though, he always had resounding success.

They ended up in an enclave of sorts that overlooked a massive arena. The desert air invaded his nostrils, and he remembered why he hated coming out here so much.

An old, gray demon with a hunched posture approached the two of them. A large sword is strapped to his back, bound in bandages. The blade seemed to weigh down the demon. He looked up at them with a pained look in his eyes.

"To what do we owe the pleasure?" he asked.

"Step aside, Pazuzu," the Sorcerer said. "Our business is not with you."

"So be it," Pazuzu said, bowing.

He stepped aside, and they made their way towards the man in the back sitting on a large stone chair. A bald man was sitting in one of the chairs as a spectator to the arena. There was a musical note tattooed to the side of his head.

"Oh, shit," he exclaimed excitedly. "This is gonna be good. I love this place."

A large man sat next to him awkwardly. The small chairs were much too small for his massive body. He has long, wild hair and a scar in the shape of a Z on his face.

"Who are they, Kryptone?" he asked rather nervously.

"Don't be stupid, man," Kryptone replied. "That's our king, dumbass."

"Sorry, brother," the big man apologized worriedly.

"You worry me, Zigrone," the bald man replied.

Barbatos approached the man who was lazily sprawled out over a large chair in the back. He has long, dark hair and is wearing a billowing cloak. The Sorcerer cleared his throat loudly to make their presence known. The man sat up with an annoyed expression.

"I could hear you breathing, Sorcerer," he said, annoyed. "What the hell do you want?"

"We need to talk," Barbatos stated.

The man took a better look at the armored man in front of him. It was starting to dawn on him who he was.

"Well, shit," he said, surprised. "It's not every day that the king stands before me."

"Things have changed," the king replied.

"I figured killing Darkus would simplify things for you. One less traitor to worry about."

"I don't care about that. His death is meaningless to me. Something more pressing has been brought forward."

"Interesting. I now see how you view your subjects. It doesn't look too good for them."

"The other elder demon is dead."

The man raised an eyebrow. This news didn't seem to bother him in the slightest.

"And?" he asked, unconcerned.

"He was killed by a couple of pitiful mortals. You should take this more seriously!"

"Why should I?"

"Dedalia is with them."

The man rose off the chair with a serious expression on his face. His facade from earlier had all but faded away.

"You should have opened with that," he said. "That changes everything."

He clapped his hands together loudly and rubbed them against each other excitedly.

"Finally! I have a reason to initiate my Shadow Games!"

"How is **that** taking this seriously?" Barbatos asked.

"These are no ordinary games," he said. "Few are ever so lucky to walk away from my games."

"You know why we're really here, Maker," the Sorcerer interjected.

The Maker rolled his eyes in disappointment. He strolled past them hastily and stopped at the edge of the enclave. He looked down at the arena.

"You two are no fun," he said in quiet disappointment. "Of course, I know why you are here. You wanna know the status of your precious army. After all, none of you can do what I can. My Maker magic is the only way to create your soldiers. Go ahead and take a good look at all the work I've done in the past couple of years."

The two of them joined him at the balcony, looking down into the arena. They wondered how they hadn't noticed it before. Demons were everywhere. They were crammed into the seats encircling the arena. Even more of them stood in the center of the arena, seemingly awaiting their command.

"There you go," the Maker said. "One hundred thousand demons strong."

"It will have to do," Barbatos sighed. "Once Roy and his misfits are all dead, then we will take Earth by force."

"You don't seem all that grateful. Do you have any idea of the time and energy I wasted putting this army of yours together?"

"No," the king said coldly. "Nor do I care."

"It would seem even we elders aren't free of your iron fist," he commented.

The Sorcerer shot him a nasty look. "Watch yourself, Maker. Do not forget your worth."

"I have something better than basic demon foot soldiers anyway."

Barbatos turned towards him, and his expression had softened slightly.

"I am intrigued," he said. "Show me."

"Gladly," the Maker said, grinning.

The Sorcerer didn't like where this was going.

# CHAPTER 22

# THE MAKER'S MONSTERS

"Follow me," the Maker said gleefully.

There seemed to be a pep in his step as he escorted them through the twisting corridors of the arena. He was very fond of the monsters that he was about to show them.

"You really shouldn't encourage him," the Sorcerer said to the king as they briskly followed after him.

"I am curious what he could possess that would be more useful than a demon," Barbatos replied.

"Knowing him," he said. "It's probably nothing more than a sham. You know that we can't trust him."

"There's only one way that we can find out."

They passed through the dungeon, and four survivors sat in their cells. Two survivors were in each cell, and their enclosures faced one another. Each of them had been the last of their kind when Chaos wiped out their respective planets. If not for the intervention of Michael, they would now be dead. They owed much to Michael, as many others did. The Maker's Shadow is what brought them here to sulk in their own misery.

The biggest of them was a half-giant. He has spiky red hair and a goatee that spirals around his mouth. His naked torso showed off his bulging muscles. His lower half is adorned with a piece of armor that hangs down from his waist. A cloth flowed from the back of his armor. A large battle hammer leaned against the wall next to him. He watched the Maker stroll down the hall happily.

"That's not good," he said. "I've never seen him so happy about **anything**."

In the cell opposite him sat a woman wearing a hooded robe. The hood did little to reveal that she was in fact an elf. Her ears stuck out from the sides of the hood in a glaring way. A bow leaned against the wall next to her. The bowstring seemed to be aglow, while the bow itself had runes etched along its surface. She sat against the wall with her head hung down low.

"The end times are probably closer than we think," she said gloomily.

A man with long blonde hair sat across from her. He has a thick golden beard, while his hair is a disheveled mess. He is wearing a faded brown jacket and torn jeans. A sword was lying on the ground next to him. It seems to give off a beautiful blue light.

"Whatever is to happen will happen soon," he said.

A man was sitting across from the half-giant. His hair is spiked up in the front, and he is wearing a long leather jacket. He has an eyepatch placed over his right eye. A long spear sat next to him, the tip stretched out into the shape of a pair of horns. He glanced down the hall at the three men strolling down the hall.

"I hope you're right, Arthur," he said. "It's so painfully dull in this place. Sure would be nice to stretch our legs for once."

"I know I'm right," Arthur said. "I don't know how I know it, but I can feel it."

***

The Maker led the king down steps that led into the depths of the dungeon. This dungeon was different from the one they had just passed through. It was equipped to deal with the monsters within.

They were greeted by a Shadow in the shape of a bald man. Unlike a man, his eyes glowed a brilliant red. He was as far from human as they come.

"Master," he said in a whispery voice upon seeing the Maker. "You have returned."

"What is this thing?" Barbatos asked, looking rather disgusted by its appearance.

"It's my Shadow," the Maker said. "You don't have one? They make excellent bodyguards."

"You praise me too much," the Shadow said, bowing his head.

"Seems trained well enough," the Sorcerer observed.

"Don't underestimate him," the Maker replied. "I could have him kill you in but a moment."

The Sorcerer noticed the Shadow following his movements with his red eyes. Still, he was relaxed, unbothered.

"I am familiar with Shadows," the Sorcerer said.

"I should have known. You are a great sorcerer, or so I am told."

They reached the first cell and could tell that it wasn't the typical cage. Its walls were made of rock from the cave itself. It had no iron bars but a powerful seal instead. A large glyph barred the way out for any monstrosity contained within.

Barbatos was impressed. He wasn't sure what he had been expecting, but it certainly wasn't this.

"How did you even craft cells like these?" he asked.

"A maker never gives away his secrets," the Maker said, grinning.

Even the Sorcerer couldn't quite fathom how he had managed to make such a structure.

"Now keep in mind this is just one type of my monsters," the Maker explained. "I can create many more monsters if you desire. But I have four other monsters to show you apart from this one."

"Well, you certainly have my attention," Barbatos said.

"I don't like this," the Sorcerer whispered in his ear.

"Be quiet," he whispered back.

The Sorcerer scowled but fell back.

"Would you like to see it?" the Maker asked excitedly.

"Why else would we be here?" the Sorcerer blurted out.

Barbatos shot him a sideways glance.

"Tsk, tsk, so impatient," the Maker said.

The Sorcerer glared at him. The Maker had no idea of the horrible things that the Sorcerer could do to him. The Maker ignored the Sorcerer's disdainful stare and placed his hand on the wall next to the seal. The glyph faded, and they could see the monster that was stowed away inside. Both Barbatos and the Sorcerer were startled. Instantly, the Sorcerer pointed his staff at the Maker.

"You intend to release your monster on us!" the Sorcerer shouted in a panic.

"Relax, fucknut," the Maker said. "The gate is still perfectly intact. I simply made the glyph transparent so you can actually see what is inside this thing."

The monster looked like a bipedal dog with human-like features. It looked at them with ruby-colored eyes. Four arms protruded from its body instead of a natural two. Its fur is matted in a dismal black. The monster in front of them has a rather muscular build. A pointed tongue lolled out of its mouth, and it was drooling onto the cave floor.

"What is that thing?" the Sorcerer asked, disgusted.

The monster growled at him angrily.

"That **thing** is a Calline," the Maker replied. "Also, it can see you and hear you. Just so you know."

"I don't care if it can," he said. "If it tries anything, I will put it out of its misery."

"No, you won't," Barbatos sighed.

"The Calline has enhanced speed and strength," the Maker said. "Making it a rather versatile foe."

"Good to know," the Sorcerer replied.

He gripped his staff tightly as they made their way around the cell. He could feel the Calline's ruby eyes watching him as he passed. Soon they reached another cell. This cell housed a large lizardman who was sitting on the cold floor. The Maker pressed against the wall to allow them to see inside. The Lizardman stood up to at least seven feet. Its scales were an emerald hue over a massive frame. It looked upon them with yellow eyes. Spikes trailed down its body from its head to the tip of its tail. It flicked its tongue at them as it noticed them analyzing him.

"This is what I call a Lizael," the Maker said.

"It's nothing more than a Lizardman," the Sorcerer scowled, rolling his eyes.

The Lizael glared at him and lifted his axe. It didn't seem to like the comparison.

"Easy, my friend," the Maker soothed him.

The Lizael snarled but then sat back down onto the floor. Still, it kept a sharp eye on the Sorcerer.

"That would be an insult to a Lizael, magic man," he continued. "They are prideful creatures. They are far superior to a typical Lizardman. Just saying anything else would be a blow to their pride. That comparison has gotten many of your demons killed. Maybe if they were a bit smarter, then your army would be a bit bigger."

They continued to a third cell. The Maker pushed against the wall to reveal the monster inside.

"This is where they get more interesting," he said, grinning.

"What the fuck?" the Sorcerer gasped.

The monster was a hybrid creature. Its upper half is that of a strong, bald man with pale gray skin. The man's arms are folded across his chest, and his eyes are shut tight. His lower body is that of a spider. Each leg is thicker than an average man's arm.

"You like my Arachnoi?" the Maker asked.

"Hell no!" the Sorcerer exclaimed. "But why are its eyes closed?"

"Trust me," he chuckled. "You don't want to know."

They continued onward to the fourth cell. The Maker revealed the monster within. This one appeared to be more of a demon than the other monsters had been.

"I thought these were your monsters?" the Sorcerer inquired. "This looks to be a high-ranking demon. Not anything original that you would have made."

It is a feminine demon with skin of a pale white. Her hair burned in a fiery red, while her eyes seemed to be an endless void. She wore dark armor that showed off much of her toned body. A pair of onyx-colored horns cradled her long, flowing hair.

"Where are you from, girl?" the Sorcerer asked her.

"I was stolen from Lucifer's Legion!" she barked.

The fury seemed to radiate off her. She was ready to kill them all. They were lucky that the seal was doing its job. She was holding the battered hilt of a sword in her hand. She grazed her sharp fingernails along its surface, and a stream of fire burst forth from it in the shape of a blade.

"This fool would be at my master's mercy if not for this damned cell!"

"You're an Erinyes, aren't you?" Barbatos questioned.

Barbatos turned towards the Maker. "Did you steal from Lucifer? Do you wish to doom us all?"

"I assure you, I did no such thing," the Maker replied rather nervously.

The look that Barbatos gave him seemed grim indeed. Almost as if fear was hidden behind his eyes. The Maker had heard stories of a terrifying demon named Lucifer but was surprised by just how much the king seemed to be terrified of him.

"The demon is lying to us then?"

"What other explanation can there be? Next cell?"

"I hope you're right. For all of our sakes."

They reached the final cell. The monster contained within did look like a demon, but it didn't appear to be anything that would be a part of Lucifer's Legion. It could definitely be one of the Maker's creations. The demon had a skin of stone. A ragged cloak was wrapped around him with horns that stretched out of his head in perfectly straight lines. The demon stared out at them with sea-blue eyes.

"Did you make this thing out of a pile of rocks?" the Sorcerer inquired.

"I am Vicana," the demon spoke. "I would break you for the insult toward my master, if not for this seal."

"Seems to be quite taken with you."

"Easy now," the Maker said. "We're just observing today. He will learn of your power soon enough."

"Very well, master," the Vicana said.

"So, you think that these abominations will make a difference for the low numbers of my army?" Barbatos asked him.

"Absolutely," the Maker said confidently.

Barbatos grabbed the Maker's shoulders and looked him in the eyes with a grim expression.

"It's not even close," he said.

"What?" the Maker asked in shock.

"If we were to invade Earth at this point, we would be severely outnumbered."

"How is that possible?"

"You would send one hundred thousand demons to their deaths. We would be facing billions of humans. How are those good odds? Even with our demons' overwhelming strength, our forces wouldn't stand a chance."

"I-I had no idea," the Maker stammered.

He hadn't expected such numbers to be thriving on Earth. He knew that there would be a lot more than they had here. But that was an entirely different level than he had been anticipating. He didn't know what to say.

"Now I wish to show you what just a small group of humans can do," Barbatos said. "The same ones that killed our good friend, Baelor."

# Chapter 23

# The Demon Slayer

The Sorcerer grabbed the shoulders of both Barbatos and the Maker, and they vanished in a darkened poof. The three of them appeared in the muddy wasteland behind the Commander's mansion. This is the battlefield where Baelor had met his end. The large pile of ash drew their attention. The only thing that remained of him was a singular horn, but even now it was crumbling to ash along with the rest of the pile behind it.

The Maker stood there, gasping in shock. He knew that Baelor was dead, but actually seeing it was something else entirely. He felt tears stinging his eyes. Baelor had been practically a brother to him. He could feel his emotions start to spiral.

"So, who's the son of a bitch who did this?" he asked, balling his hands into fists. His balled hands shook in anger.

"That would have been me," a man's voice said from behind them.

They all whirled around in surprise. They didn't think that anyone else would still be here. Jake was leaning against the mansion with his arms folded across his chest. He knew how powerful the three men in front of him were, but he just didn't care.

"Do you have any idea who you're fucking with?!" the Maker shouted at him.

"Yep," he said. "I sure do. The thing is, you're not gonna do a damn thing. You're only here to observe, right?"

"How the hell do you know that?" Barbatos questioned.

A swirling sphere of light formed on the wall behind him. A hand reached out from the light and gripped his shoulder.

"I'd tell ya, but it looks like my ride is here. Be seeing you soon, Lazeras."

The hand dragged him through the portal, and it vanished as quickly as it had appeared.

"Who the hell was that?" the Maker asked.

"That was Jake Slayon," Barbatos replied. "Among the humans, he is known as a legendary demon slayer."

"Eh, I'm not impressed," he replied.

"If you ever see that man again, do not underestimate him. He is smart as well as vicious."

"But—"

"Do **not**. Underestimate him. There is supposed to be a lesson in this."

"Which is?" the Maker asked skeptically.

"I figured you would be blind to it," Barbatos said disappointedly. "If we continue going after Roy Darsetts and his friends, then we will encounter him again. He will not go easy on us either. We will have to be ready for such an outcome. Else you will share Baelor's fate."

"I can handle myself. I have monsters to protect me."

"That's what Baelor thought, too. You weren't the only one with monsters, Maker. Now send him back, Sorcerer."

"Yes, milord," the Sorcerer said.

He placed a hand on the Maker's shoulder, and he was whisked away to his arena in an instant. He took comfort in the familiar surroundings. But then he remembered everything that he had learned. Roy Darsetts was more of a threat than he imagined. He and his friends would have to be stopped no matter what. Rage began to flood his face.

***

Jake had been taken to a cave. He had been here only a handful of times. It was a place that only made itself known when the Portalkeeper had chosen to interfere with your life. It is usually something that happens when things go well off the rails. He couldn't get over how impressive the place was. He knew that the Portalkeeper had managed to turn this cave into a livable home. The Portalkeeper had brought him here for a reason. What that may be was still up in the air. The Portalkeeper has complete control over the portals scattered across the universe. If he wanted to, he could even make new ones.

The Portalkeeper was the one who had brought him here. Now he stepped aside to allow him entry. There was another man here as well. This caught Jake by surprise. Not many are lucky enough to witness this place, much less live in it. The man has short, black hair. Currently, he isn't wearing a shirt, and sweat is glistening down his muscular frame. He was savagely punching a floating punching bag that was suspended impossibly. It was only possible due to the Portalkeeper's magic.

The man seemed to be getting out of breath, but he seemed motivated to go on. He gave it one last punch, and it was thrown across the cave floor. He glanced over at the two of them.

"Done already?" the man asked, wiping sweat from his brow.

"Darkus, we have a guest," the Portalkeeper said, throwing him his shirt.

"I see that," Darkus replied, sliding his shirt over his sweat-glistened body. "Who are you?"

"I could ask you the same thing," Jake replied skeptically.

"Name's Darkus," he said. "Dedalia's older brother. I also helped Roy out in the battle with the Lieutenant."

"Ahh, so that was you then. I am grateful to you. I wasn't able to help them, even though I wanted to, because my tech wasn't quite ready yet. I am Jake Slayon, a slayer of demons and things even more sinister."

"Based on everything that has happened, we all need to have a chat," the Portalkeeper said.

"Why did you need both of us?" Jake asked.

"As careful as I am, the Sorcerer is still onto me," he replied. "Sadly, I can't bring Darkus to a new hideout. He will notice. I need you to find a way to keep him busy."

"I don't have time for that shit."

"**Make** time for that shit. Darkus has an important role coming in the near future."

"I do?" Darkus asked, surprised.

"Don't worry too much about it. This is why I've been having you train."

"I already have another elder demon to track, and you want me to keep the Sorcerer busy on the side?" Jake asked. "How the hell am I supposed to protect him at the same time? I don't even know this guy."

He slowly turned towards Darkus and his blank face.

"No offense," he said.

"I'll be honest, I don't exactly know how I feel about you protecting me either. But if the Portalkeeper says it's the best option, then I'll trust him."

"You seem to put a lot of faith in him."

"He did save my life. **Twice**."

"I know you'll figure something out," the Portalkeeper said. "I know you can do this."

"That's not the fucking point!" Jake shot back.

"I wish you luck."

He formed a portal with the wave of his hand.

"But now I need you to leave," the Portalkeeper said. "I have to figure out a way to clean up this mess."

"Of course," Jake said, irritated. "Good luck, Darkus. If you need my help, come find me at the Secret Society. I know you know where it is. You fought the armies of Chaos there, after all."

Jake stepped through the portal. Leaving the two of them behind in the cave.

"He **did** remember me," Darkus said approvingly.

***

Jake wound up back on the muddy wasteland from before. It seemed the demon royalty had abandoned this place while he was gone. Good riddance. He would rather not encounter them again for some time if he could help it. He knew he would eventually encounter them again, but at that point, he would be trying to kill them.

"The Portalkeeper is out of his fucking mind," he said to himself.

He felt a new Portoball in his vest pocket and knew that the Portalkeeper must have snuck it there, as he had pulled him through the portal in the first place. He plucked it out of his pocket and pressed the button, feeling as if he knew where it would take him. Just as he had expected, he had been taken to the Secret Society headquarters. He was now standing a short distance away from the computer that he had used to come to Roy's aid. He sighed and wandered over to the chair at the desk. He plopped into the chair, and his eyes widened at what he was seeing on the screen.

He had been expecting to track down the other elder demon, Lazeras, but instead, a different name was blaring on the screen in front of him. It was a name he had never encountered, and he didn't think he had ever seen it in the Secret Society's database before. It calculated that the demon was even stronger than Chaos. He had always thought that Chaos was the strongest demon in the universe. None of this should be possible. But still it stood there as an eyesore. The demon is named Lucifer.

Darkus had appeared behind him, probably sent here through one of the Portalkeeper's infinite portals. He looked at the screen quizzically over Jake's shoulder. He seemed just as perplexed as Jake was.

"Who is Lucifer?" he asked curiously.

"I don't have any idea," Jake sighed nervously. "That's the fucking problem."

# CHAPTER 24

# DEVIL'S QUARREL

On a planet vastly different from Earth or even Khais, an Archdemon stumbled down a barren wasteland. Like many other demons in this place, he was human at one point. However, upon his death, his soul was claimed by an incredibly powerful entity and brought to this place. He was a terrible person in his life. If he had been a better person, he would have become a simple imp. If he had been even worse, there was an even worse demon that he would have become. The ground is a searing, rocky surface, while the sky emits a crimson glow. The demon had fear dancing in his eyes as he ran across the brimstone. This place is the planet of demons. This is Hell.

***

The events that transpired not too long ago are what put the demon into a panicked frenzy. Groups of powerful demons were marching across the landscape. These demons were soldiers of Lucifer's Legion. Few could withstand the overwhelming power of this formidable army.

Much of the army was comprised of a being called an Erinyes. A pale, feminine demon wielding a flaming sword.

This all happened during another typical day on Hell. A large group of Erinyes was making its trek down the desolate land. A Shadow appeared in a burst of darkness. He was up to no good. He served as the Maker's right hand. He knew that his master needed more monsters for his games, but the Maker was running out of ideas. He figured it wouldn't matter where they came from. His master would be pleased by his efforts. He just knew it.

"I will bring you a trophy," the Shadow promised.

He had concealed himself behind a large stalagmite of rock. Now he stepped out from behind it and waded over to the organized Erinyes. The one furthest in the back of the marching mass turned around to face the Shadow. She was well aware of his presence.

"You are a fool indeed," she snarled. "Would you endure the wrath of me and my sisters?"

"Take another look," the Shadow replied nonchalantly.

She turned around and saw that the other Erinyes were nowhere to be found.

"What magic is this?" she asked, perplexed.

"This is my magic," the Shadow whispered. "It is illusion magic. I made it seem as if you had never left their ranks, while I had actually teleported you far away from them in but an instant. Now we can talk in peace."

"Who the hell are you?"

"I am but a humble Shadow in service to my master."

"Who is this master of yours? I would report him to Lord Lucifer at once!"

"Now, now. There will be no need for that."

The Shadow burst apart in a poof of darkness and formed a large hand. The hand quickly clenched itself around the Erinyes.

"Shit!" she screamed.

She had hoped that even though the other Erinyes were so far away, maybe just one of them would be able to hear her scream. Alas, it seemed that the scream fell upon deaf ears, as not one of them turned around. She felt that her luck had been cursed as she was whisked away from Hell. Not once had she ever left Hell, and she wasn't sure if she liked it. The brutish atmosphere was comforting to her. Now she was being thrust into a place that she didn't know against her will.

***

The Shadow had brought her to the deepest depths of the dungeon below the Maker's arena. He deposited her into an empty cell and pressed the groove to activate the seal. She had tried to escape before the seal could activate, but the powerful magic threw her back into the cell with a strong spark. Steam billowed off her as she sat against the back wall of the cell.

The Shadow smiled at her, even though it was difficult to see on his shadowy face. "My master will be most pleased."

"When Lord Lucifer finds out what you have done, death will feel sweet compared to what he will put you through," she promised.

"That is of no consequence," the Shadow whispered.

Then he left her in the room. Her eyes wandered around the room, memorizing the features. Several monsters were in the other cells. They looked horrific, and she didn't feel comfortable being trapped in the same room as them. She was in here with a bunch of freaks. It was rather unsettling. Being grouped with such monsters felt like a bit of an insult. It just showed her what people really thought of her.

"Whoever this master of his is will be in deep shit," she said. "Next time I see my Lord Lucifer, I will be sure to tell him of everything that has happened here. I'll just need to find out the bastard's name."

***

Back on Hell, an Archdemon had been behind another stalagmite. This demon had seen everything that the Shadow had done. He watched in horror as the Erinyes was taken away from her kin. This is the same demon that is now stumbling across a valley of brimstone. He needed to inform his boss. His boss is the one in charge of the demons within Lucifer's Legion. Belial, Lord of the Imps.

"I just gotta reach him before he finds out from someone else," he panted. "He already told me one more fuck-up and I'll be getting a beheading."

He sprinted across a wobbly, wooden bridge. The only reason the bridge wasn't in shambles was due to a powerful magic that protected it from the insufferable heat in this place. The Archdemon nearly fell into the stone building on the other side. He ran into an even bigger demon than him. Archdemons are already considered large, but this demon made him look small.

He looked up at the demon he had just run into with a nervous glance. He was at least two feet taller than him with even more muscle. His ashy, gray skin is riddled with scars. The demon in front of him has an extra pair of arms that he knew he would never possess. Two of his arms are folded across his chest, while the other two hang at his side in standby. This creature is referred to as a Kaiser Demon. They are the vanguard of Lucifer's Legion. Almost no one would ever hope to compete with their strength. They were all trained by Lucifer himself. All of them meet his high standards.

The demon stared down at him menacingly. "I hope you have a good reason for running into me like a hopeless drunk."

The Archdemon chuckled nervously. "Just here to see our lord. I have important information for him."

"Then by all means," the Kaiser Demon gestured. "But may I suggest using the front door?"

"Right," the Archdemon said, shuffling past him.

He gulped anxiously before he strolled into the building. It looked like it was an average place. The interior resembled that of a typical house, but the entire structure was made of stone, and a throne was awkwardly placed in its center. The king who sat upon it was clearly disrespected by the one who had given him his position. A rounded crimson rug sat underneath the legs of the cheap throne. A demon sat upon the throne, barely supporting his weight. He was the one that the Archdemon had been searching for.

This demon had rusty-colored scales and wouldn't stand much taller than the Archdemon in front of him. Still, he gave off the feeling of importance. His horns were smaller, and he had a long, bulbous nose. A large pair of wings was folded up on his back, making his current position look rather uncomfortable. He gazed upon the Archdemon with blackened eyes. The demon sitting on the throne was clutching a trident in his right hand. It had signs of clear use, staining its long frame. This demon is the Lord of the Imps, Belial.

"Why are you here, scrub?" Belial asked him.

"I-I have news," the Archdemon stammered.

"Well, spit it out then," he urged him rather impatiently.

"One of the Erinyes were taken."

Belial sprang to his feet with the trident still in his hand. The throne nearly fell over as he did so. He stared at the Archdemon unblinking as he stared intensely upon the cowering demon in front of him.

"What?!" he shouted furiously. "By whom?!"

"It was a Shadow," the Archdemon muttered.

Belial had somehow understood the Archdemon over his pathetic whimper. So, a Shadow was responsible. He would just need to find it and destroy it before things got any more out of hand.

"Are you absolutely certain?" he asked.

"I saw the whole thing," the Archdemon said, trembling.

"Shit!" Belial screamed in a rage.

He chucked the trident at the Archdemon, and the demon was thrown into the wall behind him. He was held up by the trident jutting out of the wall. The Kaiser Demon from outside wandered inside and saw the sorry state of the Archdemon, whom he had run into before. He knew that he was treated as the weakling that he was.

"All the Archdemons are utterly useless," Belial growled as he wandered to the hanging demon. "It's any wonder that I keep any of them around."

He gripped his trident and pried it out of the Archdemon's torso. The demon's body collapsed onto the stone floor. Then he turned towards the Kaiser Demon.

"Feed him to the snakes," he ordered. "If anyone asks, I'm not here."

"Yes, milord," the Kaiser Demon said, bowing to him.

Belial left the building, and the Kaiser Demon watched him run to the edge of the riverbank to the steady stream of lava. Belial leapt into the air and flapped off into the distance. The Kaiser Demon knew that he would be heading to the palace in the distance. He quietly wished him luck, as the demons there were even worse than they were here. The Kaiser Demon looked down at the corpse of the Archdemon.

"Imbecile," he sighed.

Then he plucked the Archdemon off the floor as if he were nothing more than a pillow. He hoisted the demon's body onto his shoulders and carried him outside. He reached the edge of the cliff and looked down at the river of lava far below them. He hurled the Archdemon down into the river. The demon's body hit the lava and floated there instead of sinking into its depths.

Then a large snake's mouth burst through the lava and devoured the demon whole. It stretched its body so that its head was a few feet away from the Kaiser Demon. It flicked its pronged tongue at the demon. Its bright blue eyes seemed to glow as they peered out at him. Dark stripes trailed its body, with spikes lining its frame. He was waiting for it to try something, but then it dove back into the lava below.

"Hell Snakes," the Kaiser Demon grunted. "They never seem to know their place."

Hell Snakes had a strong appetite for demons, making it easier to keep the demons in line in this place. The King of Hell used this to his advantage, so he had complete control over his subjects. No one would dare to defy him due to all the Hell Snakes.

The Kaiser Demon then returned to his post just outside Belial's house. He could only ponder if any more excitement would be coming his way.

***

Everything beneath Belial seemed to be nothing more than a blur as he flew on past. The one thing that would worry him is how Lucifer reacted upon hearing of the loss of one of his precious Erinyes. He is a rather meticulous man who didn't like anything out of his control. The loss of just one of his many soldiers could send him over the edge. Belial landed at a thin brimstone bridge that led up into Lucifer's Palace. He begrudgingly crossed the bridge and stepped toward the entrance to the palace.

Belial strode past a pair of Kaiser Demons that guarded the entrance. They recognized him and didn't even give him a second glance. Being the right hand to Lucifer certainly had its perks. He made his way through the many halls of the palace. Eventually he found Lucifer's room. He swung the door open urgently.

"For fuck's sake!" an angry man shouted.

He had forgotten about Lucifer's rather erotic tendencies with the ladies. He was lying on his bed with a woman underneath his sheets, while two intoxicatingly beautiful feminine demons lay naked on either side of him. They had pale gray skin and large black horns reaching out from their heads, confining their long wavy hair. These demons are Succubus, creatures that feed ravenously on lust. Lucifer was the kind of man who would be able to keep them occupied for some time.

The two Succubus lying beside him were waiting for their turn to follow the Succubus who was currently giving Lucifer some sensual service. He did have quite the way with the ladies. He looked as if he had been enjoying himself before Belial had arrived. Now that moment was ruined.

"Does anyone ever knock around here?" he asked. "Maybe pay attention to the fucking sign on the door?"

Belial noticed there was indeed a sign that he had accidentally ripped off the doorknob. It read, *do not disturb*. Who would have guessed?

"My apologies," Belial apologized, bowing his head.

"Give me a fucking minute!" Lucifer shouted at him, feeling his pleasure reaching its limits. "You can wait outside!"

Belial left the room and closed the door behind him. Then he leaned against the wall. He knew what they were doing based on the echoing moans of pleasure muffled by the wall behind him. Then suddenly it stopped. Belial was curious. Did he really satisfy all three of them in five minutes? Surely not.

"Be back in a moment, my lovelies," Lucifer said from behind the wall.

The three of them sounded disappointed. He had no idea how Lucifer managed to charm all three of them so effectively. Sadly, he didn't have the time to question it. Lucifer had already kicked the door open and was glaring at Belial intensely.

The man has spiky dark hair and is wearing a leather jacket, unzipped, showing off his fit physique. His jeans looked worn beyond their time. He has a ring on each hand, each in the shape of a demon's head. The man peered at him with smoldering red eyes that seemed to gaze through his very soul.

"I hope you have a damn good reason for disturbing my **me** time," Lucifer growled at him.

"You're not gonna like this," Belial murmured.

The fact that Belial spoke so quietly only irritated him more. It was rather similar to the Archdemon he had dealt with not so long ago.

"Well, what is it?" he snarled. "Speak up and tell me."

"One of your Erinyes has been taken, sir."

Lucifer's eyes seemed to burn even brighter.

"So, you let someone steal from me?!" he inquired angrily. "Do they even know who I am?! This will not bode well for my reputation! You realize that, yes?!"

"Yes," Belial sighed.

"What the hell are you fucktwits even doing?! How hard is it to keep a fucking army intact?!"

"There wasn't much we could do, sir. It was all the work of some Shadow. Even if we had encountered him, there wouldn't be much we could do to stop him."

The understanding dawned on Lucifer's face. He knew of only one person who even had a Shadow in his employ. A free-roaming Shadow wouldn't be stupid enough to steal from him. He knew the Maker was behind this; whether he was aware of it himself was yet to be determined. He slowly calmed down to a silent frustration. The rage still simmered at his surface, but there was only one option left to him in this situation.

"A Shadow, huh? I should have known. Few other beings would be able to pull off something quite like this. It would seem the Maker is stupid enough to steal from me after all. I'll kill the bastard."

He grabbed the pronged tip of the trident in Belial's hand and dragged him down the hall. "Come along now, Belial."

Belial looked scared. He knew where Lucifer was taking him. The throne room where the King of Hell sat. He had never met the king, but the rumors of his horrible ruthlessness made him rather nervous.

"It's about time that my brother does something about these troublesome Immortals. I have had enough of their bullshit."

If this were in better circumstances, Belial might not have felt so much fear as they got closer to the throne room. He couldn't shake the feeling that whatever happened, he would be dragged into it as well. It felt like an ill omen.

Lucifer kicked open the tall doors barring their way forward. He dragged Belial with him into the throne room. The room itself looked more like an exquisite hallway than a king's room. They strolled down a blue carpet stretched to the malicious-looking throne in the back of the room. Alongside them there were statues with torches clutched in their hands. Each of the torches was alight with an ominous green flame. Suits of armor stood in the back of the room alongside the throne where a man sat. Finally, they reached the man that Lucifer had come seeking an audience with. His older brother, Satan.

The throne on which he sat was jagged, with several spikes jutting out from it. It is coated in an obsidian hue.

A large, spiked sword was jabbed into the floor in front of Satan. Satan held onto the hilt of the sinister blade as he looked upon them. It was rather intimidating. But it made it easy for him to quickly deal with any troublesome guests. Rather fitting on a chaotic planet such as this.

The man wore dark, tattered robes and had a ring on nearly every finger. His long, wavy dark hair matched his long beard, which seemed to billow in the air. His fiery red eyes seemed to judge them as he glanced upon them. He seemed as powerful and fear-inducing as Belial had heard.

Lucifer released the tip of Belial's trident, and the Lord of Imps nearly fell to the floor in front of him in surprise. His nervousness was blatantly obvious.

"What is the meaning of this, little brother?" Satan asked him.

That struck a chord with Lucifer. He did not enjoy being referred to as the little brother. Even Belial could tell that much. It showed on Lucifer's now twitching face.

"I grow tired of these Immortals doing whatever they please, brother," Lucifer said with a twinge of annoyance. "It's time to put them in their fucking place!"

Satan sighed. "That's what this outburst is all about? We will do no such thing. We do not have time for a war against the Immortals. They are simply doing as fate wills it."

"What the fuck is it that you're so scared of, brother?!" he asked angrily.

"They are doing what they are deemed to do. I will not disgrace fate for your misguided tantrum."

"Fuck that! You're the fucking Lord of Hell! You can do whatever the hell you want! Who cares what fate has decided?!"

"I **am** doing what I want. You will not be the one to twist my mind."

Lucifer could sense a danger behind Satan's calm tone. But he kept pushing. He would not be deterred by Satan's ominously quiet voice.

"If you won't do it, brother, then I will!" Lucifer threatened.

"And what of your friend here?" Satan asked, pointing out Belial quivering on the ground.

"Of course, he agrees with me," Lucifer said, deciding for him. "He will be the one helping me to eradicate the Immortals."

Satan's eyes shifted between the two of them. He didn't seem to be convinced by Lucifer's lies.

"Spare me your lies, brother," Satan said. "I know that this demon next to you is but a sacrificial pawn. You have told me as such quite often."

Belial couldn't believe what he was hearing. He knew that Lucifer thought lowly of him. But now he knew just how low he had thought of him. It was quite a shock to him. Being his right hand, he was still treated as nothing more than a worthless waste of space.

"But it seems you will not listen to reason," Satan sighed. "So, I will have to have my guest take care of you."

"Guest?" Lucifer asked, amused. "Since when?"

There was a burst of gray energy behind Lucifer, and it formed into a man wearing thick silver armor. The bald man in armor towered over him, and he couldn't help but feel as if he had seen the armored man before. The man gazed down at Lucifer with shining silver eyes. A cool blue cloak is wrapped around his neck that billowed around him. The armor was short enough for his rippling muscles to be on display.

"Who the hell are you?" Lucifer asked.

"I am the Lightbringer," the man said. "I am the goodness of Chaos' soul."

"How sickening," he scowled. "Everything always comes back to Chaos."

"Deal with them, my friend," Satan pleaded.

The Lightbringer grabbed Lucifer by the collar of his jacket and the pronged edge of Belial's trident. Then he lifted both of them into the air.

"Me too?" Belial asked shakily.

"You were volunteered by your gracious lord," Satan said. "I'm nothing if not agreeable."

"Fuck me," Belial sighed.

A gray cloud engulfed them as the Lightbringer had willed it.

"Motherf—" Lucifer exclaimed as the gray energy enclosed around them.

Then all of them left the room. A minute later, the Lightbringer came forth from a gray burst of energy.

"I hope he learns something from all of this," Satan sighed.

"He will have to learn **something**," the Lightbringer said. "I sent him to a world far more chaotic than our own."

"That is probably the best place for him to realize the errors of his ways," he replied. "If not, I fear I may have to be the one to put him down."

"I wouldn't worry so much, milord."

"Why not?"

"There is a prophecy by the Dark Messiah rather recently that may change his life forever."

"Prophecy?"

"The Dark Messiah has made a new one in the Void, but because she isn't in the right world, the information is wrong."

"Then there is but one thing for us to do. Find her and bring her where she belongs, my friend. The truth needs to be brought to light. Maybe then, Lucifer will fear his fate just a little bit more."

"As you wish, milord," the Lightbringer said, bowing his head.

# Chapter 25

## Banished No More

Deep in the darkest recesses of the Void, Judgement gazed down at the Dark Messiah's mangled body. He hadn't wanted to react as he did but felt that he had little choice. She had betrayed his king. Her death would serve as her punishment. Never again to defy him. He turned away from her body to calm himself. He had other things to concern himself with.

A cloud of gray formed in front of him. It formed into the shape of a man who looked similar to the Chaosbringer. But that made no sense, as he had just left this place. He shouldn't be back already.

"What do you want now?" Judgement inquired.

"I don't think you realize who it is you're talking to," the man said.

Judgement noticed that the man spoke the truth. His dark armor that he had grown accustomed to was now a gleaming silver. His bright chrome eyes seemed to travel right through him. However, his face was smooth, and the cloak around his neck was pale blue. Judgement tightened his grip on the handle of his axe.

"Who exactly are you supposed to be?" he asked.

"I am the Chaosbringer's **other** half," the man declared. "I am the Lightbringer. All of the good that was once harbored within Chaos' soul lives through me."

"So why come to a place like this?"

"I have come for the one named the Dark Messiah. She doesn't belong in this world. I have entered this dreary place to take her back to where she rightfully belongs."

Judgement turned back toward the bloody body on the ground and shook his head. This man clearly was not very good at arriving at the proper time. He would have to give the Lightbringer the bad news.

"You are a little late for that," Judgement said.

The Lightbringer peered down at the body on the ground. It was quite a mess for sure, but his expression remained unchanged.

"This means nothing," he declared. 'Enough of the games, Seer. Show yourself. It's time you went back to where you belong. This is the only way for the true prophecy to take shape. And I think you know it."

Judgement looked at him like he was crazy. The Lightbringer knew that he probably seemed to be quite insane. Still, he knew how the Dark Messiah's power worked.

"You're talking to a corpse," Judgement said in disbelief. "You realize that, don't you?"

But then the Dark Messiah appeared right next to Judgement. He stared at the elderly demon in surprise.

"What the fuck is that then?!" he asked exasperated, pointing out the bloodied body on the ground.

"Just a basic illusory double," she said. "I wanted you to be convinced that I was dead."

"For what purpose?"

"I grew tired of your ramblings. Did you really think that it would be that simple to kill me as the previous right hand of Chaos?"

"I suppose not," he sighed, hanging his head in defeat.

The Dark Messiah had outwitted him tenfold. He didn't consider himself dumb, but her intelligence had made him question it. He just didn't know how he was supposed to wrap his head around it. He should have expected as much from such a powerful demon as her. She had betrayed them all. More importantly, she had betrayed Barbatos, the Demon King. He knew that he was powerless to stop her.

The Lightbringer gently placed a hand on the Dark Messiah's shoulder. Judgement could see the differences between him and the Chaosbringer. They were entirely different people. But her calm face suddenly changed.

"I don't want to go back there," she said, snarling.

"I know you don't," the Lightbringer said calmly. "But you have been in this world long enough. You have done everything that fate has asked of you here. Now you must go back to finish what you started."

"I'm **not** going back!" she screamed.

She swiftly raised her hand, and a powerful funnel of air drilled into the Lightbringer. He stuck his feet firmly into the rocky ground, but still he slid across the platform. The force caused his feet to scrape away at the platform's surface. She lowered her hand and brought up her other hand. She shot a fireball through the palm of her hand. It burst into the Lightbringer's chest plate. He was thrown off his feet as the explosion seared into his armor.

After withstanding all her relentless attacks, there was but a single crack in the Lightbringer's armor. Now he used his own magic to levitate off the ground on a gray cloud planted beneath his feet.

"Don't do this, Seer," he warned. "It won't end well for either of us."

"You left me no choice, you damned god!" she shouted in a rage.

She lifted her hand, and a flowing streak of blue lightning zigzagged its way into his armor. His body shook wildly as he was electrocuted. The power of her magic was enhanced due to the metallic alloy of his armor. Once it finally stopped zapping him, steam rose off his body. Still, he looked calm as he gazed upon her.

"I will not harm you," he said. "But you will come to your designated place, seer."

"Never!" she shrieked.

The Dark Messiah punched the ground, and the platform trembled violently. Cracks rapidly stretched across its surface, and the outer edges began crumbling into the unforgiving Void. The dissipating destruction of the platform began to slowly reach towards its center, where Judgement stood, not even realizing the danger that he was in.

"Damn it!" the Lightbringer shouted. "Calm yourself, Seer!"

He wasn't worried about himself but knew that fate had other plans for Judgement. He couldn't allow the ancient demon to succumb to the darkness of the Void. He teleported behind Judgement and roughly wrapped his arms around the demon's body.

"You can't die here," he said. "Not yet."

Then the two of them vanished in a quick burst of gray.

***

The two of them ended up in an abandoned cavern. Stalagmites sprouted from the floor, while smaller stalactites stretched down from the ceiling. They were scattered about just enough to allow them to move comfortably through the cave. Their breathing was shallow, as the air in this place was compromised. Almost as if it were poison. A weak poison, but a poison all the same.

"What is this place?" Judgement asked.

"This is a cavern below the Demon Castle," the Lightbringer said. "Fate has much in store for you here."

Judgement was taken aback. After everything that he had done, he felt he was unworthy of being in the presence of the Demon Castle. He wasn't sure if he was being redeemed or punished.

"But why bring me here?" he asked.

"I know not what sinister plans my dark half had in store for you, but fate has its own plans for you. Fate wants you here. There will be a fixed point where you must be here in this place. I do not know the reason. Your best option is to accept it and fulfill your role."

"Whatever my role is, I'm sure that I'm not worthy of it."

"That is yet to be decided. For now, I ask that you remain here. It will be clear once the moment arrives. Just know that if you leave this place and try tracking down the heroes, I will know, and I will not be as nice as I am now."

"You don't seem to be the type."

"I assure you I will not even need to intervene if you defy your fate. It will do the job for me. After all, there are worse fates than death."

"Maybe I have earned it."

"If you wish to find out a worse fate, then go ahead and deny it. Watch what happens. I won't save you from it."

Then the Lightbringer disappeared in a poof of gray. Judgement was stunned by the prospect of his new fate. He wasn't sure what he was supposed to think of it. Looked to him like he was a last resort against Roy's ambition.

***

The Lightbringer returned to the Void, his calmness from before slowly fading away.

"Seer!" he shouted over the loud crumbling of the platform. "Enough of all this! You know what must be done!"

"I would rather **die** than go back there!" she screamed.

The platform was ripped apart and scattered into the shadowy depths of the Void. She floated in the center of a swirling storm of rubble. Then she snapped her fingers, and the debris shattered all at once. It was difficult seeing through all the dust that she had created in the air.

Then he noticed that she was using more of her magic. It was an illusion spell. She had a large number of doubles that were now floating in the air all around him. He sighed. It seemed that she was planning to pull out all the stops. All her forms opened their mouths wide, and a red glow emanated from their maws. Then each double breathed flame onto the Lightbringer's helpless body simultaneously.

He lifted his arms to better protect himself from the blazing flames from every direction. Finally, they stopped, and his armor felt like it had become much more brittle. He knew that his armor wouldn't be able to take much more of this. He needed to find a way to capture her. Still, he didn't want to hurt her.

The doubles began changing shape into a different form. He doubted that she had suddenly surrendered. He was sure she had worse plans in store for him. Each of the copies had turned into large blades. Sometimes he really hated being right. The Dark Messiah was holding her right hand high over her head.

"Nothing personal," she said. "But as I keep reminding you, I will not be returning to that horrible world."

The Lightbringer looked around at the floating swords that now encircled him. She put on quite the show, but he knew the truth. She was scared. This showed just how desperate she was to stay here in a world that she deemed safe. It didn't matter. Fate had made its choice. The balance of this world depended on her returning to the one she had come from.

She lowered her hand, and all the swords soared towards him at once. He embraced the fact that most of them would be meeting his flesh. He had little choice in the matter. Even his teleportation wouldn't do much good against that many hazards. Several of the swords pierced through his armor, while many of the others missed and became victims of the dark power of the Void. Each sword felt like a prick as it broke through his armor. If it hadn't been for the power he had inherited from Chaos, it would have been much worse.

The feeling from the sharp stinging of the blades was still enough to cause him tremendous pain. He stood strong before her. It was time to remind her why he was considered a deity. Even in this world. His silver eyes glowed brightly, and his hands clenched into fists. He folded his arms across his chest and let out a booming shout. Then a powerful light seemed to encompass his body. He swung his arms open wide, and a shockwave of light reverberated off his body, knocking all the swords off his armor. He looked up at the Dark Messiah with eyes still aglow.

"Seer!" he declared. "I do not wish to hurt you. Do not force my hand!"

"I told you I will never go back!" she shrieked.

She stretched out a shaky hand, showing how her fear was coming to light. She floated high above the Lightbringer. A strong torrent of water spun toward him. He lifted his hands up to protect himself. Gray energy made a shield around him, and he struggled to withstand the raging water as it pounded against his barrier. He felt his magic weakening. Her magic would eventually break through. He could see that he was right about her desperation.

As things were starting to look grim for him, a swirling light appeared above the Dark Messiah. It had formed into a portal. A man's hand reached through it and grabbed one of her horns.

"You will return," the voice of the Portalkeeper echoed throughout the Void.

He hurled her through her own torrent of water. The Lightbringer suddenly clapped his hands together, and it was as if he had slashed through the funnel of water crashing against him. The water split apart, and the Dark Messiah fell into his arms. Then he teleported the two of them before she had the chance to react.

# CHAPTER 26

# ANOTHER WORLD

The Lightbringer had successfully brought them out of the dark confines of the Void. A starry night sky shimmered above them. The Dark Messiah forced herself out of his grip and dropped onto the pavement. She looked up and dared not believe it. The place they were in looked like it was New York, but something about it seemed to be off.

However, two of the last people that she had wanted to see stood in front of her. She recognized one as a demon, while the other appeared as a man dressed in dark leather. She knew who they would be before they even turned around. The demon was Belial, and the man was Lucifer. The Lightbringer had brought her back to her own world. It was the same chaotic place to which Satan himself had banished Lucifer and Belial. She knew that the chaotic nature of this world would force the prophecy to become known, and this was what she was afraid of. Lucifer would not like it once she revealed its truth. They saw the two of them, and a sly smirk curled up onto

Lucifer's face. Then the both of them approached the Dark Messiah as she appeared rather squeamish in front of them. The fate of both worlds was about to change for the worse. She sat on the cold, hard ground, watching helplessly as the two continued strolling towards her.

"Do you realize what you've done?" The Dark Messiah, her voice slightly trembling with fear, asked the Lightbringer.

"I do," the Lightbringer said plainly. "I'm sorry, but it is for the best. Your fate is here."

"Back so soon, shiny man?" Lucifer asked him.

"I've only returned what belongs here."

Then he was gone in a poof of gray. Lucifer seemed rather disappointed by this.

"Well, that's just no fun," Lucifer said, saddened. "So why are **you** here then?"

He looked in the Dark Messiah's direction. She got to her knees and suddenly felt rippling pain spread throughout her body. She clutched at her chest with tears welling in her eyes from the pain's intensity. Then she shrieked in her anguish. It was happening. There was no fighting it now. The prophecy she had tried to avoid. It was about to make itself known, and there was nothing she could do to stop it.

"What the fuck is wrong with you?" he asked, raising an eyebrow.

She sat on her knees, and her body arched backwards of its own accord. It seemed unnatural, as her head was forced to look up into the dark sky above her. Her claws sunk into the pavement at her sides, and her eyes rolled into the back of her head.

"The spirits," she whispered.

"What?" Lucifer asked, stepping towards her.

Belial seemed to be nervous just looking at the Dark Messiah's twisting body. He didn't know what to think of what was happening.

"The days of Lucifer are numbered!" The Dark Messiah declared, her voice seeming to have merged with many voices at once. The spirits had taken over her completely.

The smirk on Lucifer's face quickly inverted into a snarl. His easygoing demeanor changed into irritation. Being called out like that for a trivial prophecy was not something he had been expecting.

"On this very street he will fight the one bearing the name of Darsetts!" she continued. "It will be a fight of intertwining destinies! Many will fall! Still, humanity will be the victor due to the efforts of the Darsetts family! Hell will never be the same after the death of the dreaded Lucifer!"

The Dark Messiah fell forward, leaning against the pavement, and glanced up at Lucifer. His eyes were harboring an intense rage. She understood his anger but felt small in the presence of it.

"So, you would dare to prophesize my demise?" He asked. "I'm curious, will your prophecy come true if you die in this place?"

"This is why I didn't want to come back here," she whimpered. "He forced me here. I had hoped that if I never returned here, then this prophecy would never have been born."

She stood up but felt small in the wake of Lucifer's aura. It felt as if his rage created a blistering inferno around him.

"But here you are," he said, his voice filled with quiet anger. "It's time for you to realize just how much influence I already have over this world."

"But you've only been here a couple of minutes," she said curiously.

"You would be surprised how much I can accomplish in but a few minutes," he said, smirking at her. "Now, Belial, try to kill her with that pointy stick of yours."

She noticed that his joking ways were returning to him. Still, she didn't trust it. Lucifer knew just how strong she was. This felt like more of a test than anything else. Belial flung his trident at her, and she swiped her arm through the air. A gust of wind tore into the trident, and it soared well over the demon's head. It clattered at the roadside a ways off from her two adversaries.

She didn't want to give Belial the chance to react. All that mattered right now was her own survival, and she knew that Belial was weak compared to herself. She would need to make quick work of him. She held out her hands with her palms facing up and conjured a fireball in each. She twisted her hands towards Belial, and the fireballs intensified into two steady streams of flame that engulfed the demon. He screamed in anguish as the fire charred his body.

"Let's not make things too heated," Lucifer said, smiling at her.

He reached his hand into the intense flames, and they were absorbed into his hand in seconds. It gave his hand an orange glow.

"**This** is how you use fire, bitch."

The glow got brighter before forming into a massive fireball. He fired the large fireball at her, and a powerful explosion blasted into her body. She was thrown through the window of the building behind her.

She had been wondering why this part of town had been abandoned. There hadn't been a single soul here.

No human, vehicle, monster, nothing. She didn't know it yet, but she was about to find out. The dark and empty building held some secrets. These secrets were drawn to the bloody gash that stood out on her chest.

A man and woman approached her helpless body. The man had ginger-colored hair, while the woman's dark hair was side-swept into a punk style. Their pale skin seemed to be serene to look at. They both wore long, dark coats and old jeans. Each of them wore scarves that covered their mouths. Hiding away the evidence of what they really were. If she had doubted where she was before, this only confirmed it. These monsters didn't exist in the world where Roy and the others were now.

They lowered their scarves and bared their vampiric fangs at her. Almost as if to remind her of what they were. These are the vampires of this world. They hissed at her and ran at a speed that a typical human would not be capable of. Their running appeared to be more of a glide, showcasing their elegance.

"Damn bloodsuckers," she groaned.

She used her magic to let the vampires bite into the necks of hastily crafted doubles. The vampires brought the doubles to the floor with ease and savored the taste of the blood. The true Dark Messiah stepped out of the building, leaving the ravenous vampires behind her.

"Did you enjoy the welcome party?" Lucifer asked, grinning at her.

Lucifer held a chain in each hand, and at the end of each one was a large black dog. Flickering embers raced through their matted fur. Their sinister eyes seemed to shine in a vibrant red. The Dark Messiah was not eager to find out what they would do to her if they caught her.

"Are you a dog walker now?" she asked.

"You say I've only been here but a few minutes," he said. "But I already have influence over these monsters, as you have seen. The mindless and weak monsters in Chaos' realm pale in comparison to the terrifying ones found here. Now I will stop this damned prophecy before any irritating Darsetts will ever be able to reach me."

He let go of the chains, and the large dogs sprinted in her direction.

"Get her, my Hellhounds," he ordered.

The Dark Messiah tried to run from them, but they were faster than she expected. Each of their powerful maws clamped onto her legs and dragged her onto the ground. They began gnawing on her legs as if they were bones.

She twisted her body around so that she could see the two of them more clearly. Then she launched a powerful tempest of wind at them. They whimpered as they rolled past Lucifer. He stood unfazed as the strong wind flapped his jacket. The wind seemed pathetic against his strong stature. He pointed at her with a stern look on his face. The Hellhounds rushed past him.

The Dark Messiah got back onto her feet and stretched her arms out in front of her. The air around her got cold as she squeezed her eyes shut tight. Her surroundings began to freeze as she focused on enhancing the power of her magic. This was one of the few spells she knew that took time to take effect. She swung her arms upwards, and two crystals popped into the Hellhound's bodies from below the ground. They had turned into elegant ice sculptures before death had claimed them. The sculptures turned red as their life was drained away from them.

The Dark Messiah was panting heavily. She hadn't used so much of her magic in succession in some time. Lucifer noticed this and smiled at her.

"Now that wasn't very nice," he said. "Just know, seer. You will never get away from me. No matter how desperate you become."

She gathered herself and adjusted her body to better cast more magic at the opponent in front of her. But then something happened that she had not anticipated. Something bit her shoulder. She wasn't sure what it was. But she felt her body slowly going numb. As if she no longer had any control of it. She couldn't turn her head but could see the culprit at a glance.

The creature appeared to be a man, albeit one whose flesh was rotting away. What little hair he had left hung loosely from the top of his head. Old scrapes and bruises were stuck to his decaying face. She felt that she could almost see his skull through a disgusting hole in his cheek. His eyes were yellowed and glazed over. He wore a business suit, but it was in shredded shambles.

She knew what this man was. During her time in this world, she had done everything she could to avoid creatures such as these. It was a zombie. It continued to rip and tear at her flesh. She was completely at the zombie's whim. There was nothing that she could do. Her eyes rolled back, and her body began to shake as the convergence was already taking hold.

Lucifer approached her. She wanted to break free of the zombie's grasp, but her bodily functions were failing her. Another zombie latched onto her arm and began feasting on her inviting flesh. In front of her, Lucifer paused and gazed down at her pathetic state. She had been quite the foe just a second ago, but now she had been reduced to nothing more than a husk of what she once was. She wanted to say something. **Anything**. But her mouth had betrayed her, refusing to work.

"Chaos may have taken over that reality," Lucifer said. "But this. This is **my** reality. If any of those hopeful heroes follows me here, I will burn them to fucking ash."

The Dark Messiah knew what he was about to do before it even happened. She was terrified, but all she could do was convulse as the zombie's genes took control of her mind.

"Here's a quick demonstration of what will happen to any Darsetts that dare to come to this place," he said icily.

He raised his hand, and a vortex of flame spun through Messiah's right shoulder and continued on through the zombie's head that was snacking on her scaly skin. She knew that the flame wasn't even the force of her demise. That was just how he conjured it. The flame had changed into a long, curved, and serrated blade. A weapon crafted by Lucifer himself. Capable of killing just about anything. The Dark Messiah let out a loud, guttural scream. This was the best that she could do in her zombie state. Even as a zombie, the pain was unbearable.

"If your fucking prophecy comes to light, I will burn everything down. This precious Darsetts family you cling so hopefully to will burn first. Then I will raze everything and everyone else."

Lucifer's red eyes shone in a brilliant crimson glow, and Messiah's body began to burn where the sword had entered her body. The fire spread quickly to engulf her body. Then it even spread to the two zombies munching away on her. Lucifer's eyes dulled back to their normal state, and he jerked the blade out of his victims. Their blood sprayed all over him, but it didn't bother him. This was just the beginning of his plan for this world. He was about to get a lot more blood on his hands.

The Dark Messiah joined the two zombies as a burning corpse on the pavement. Lucifer waded right through them and snapped his fingers. His sword vanished in a spark of flame.

"I know the Darsetts brothers will come for me," he said. "Maybe even the entire family. But I know that I have some time before they join hands. I relish the day that I can burn them away into dismal nothingness."

***

A hooded man stood in the shade given by a nearby alley. His chin is coated in a beard of stubble. He kept his head down, not wanting to attract any attention from such a horrific man. He peered down the street to ensure that Lucifer was well out of sight. Then he sighed in relief.

"That was too close," the man whispered grimly.

A woman stood opposite him in a dark robe with streaks of purple lined over it. She has gray hair reaching down to her shoulders. She has an eyepatch over her left eye that she didn't talk about. A single diagonal line served as a scar over that very eye.

"What is he doing here, William?" she asked.

"I wished that I knew," the man replied. "But I can assure you, Morgan, that it's nothing good. We will have to be more careful while hunting the monsters on this world. We don't want to run into him again."

"It's bound to happen eventually," Morgan replied. "We are Darsetts. He will surely find us sooner rather than later."

"We will cross that bridge when we come to it," William replied. "For now, let's quickly leave this place."

"If you insist," she agreed.

# CHAPTER 27

# THE MAKER'S DECLARATION

Back on Khais, the Maker sank into his chair. He was shown just how little he knew of the human world and just what they were capable of. It was quite a lot for him to process. He was much more wholly unprepared than he had thought. Before he found this chair to be comfortable, he watched many battles unfold in his arena. His usual lax nature dissipated, and he looked more serious. He lifted his head up to look around at everyone who had gathered here in his presence.

Kryptone glanced behind him at the Maker, and he grinned excitedly.

"Shit's about to go down!" he exclaimed.

"Shadow, come forth!" the Maker barked.

The Shadow slid up from the floor in front of the Maker. He bowed before his master humbly.

"What do you wish from me, Master?" he inquired.

"I want you to answer me honestly," the Maker said, fuming. "Did you steal from Lucifer?"

"I did."

The Maker's suddenly contorted face, now filled with anger, didn't even faze the Shadow.

"Are you out of your fucking mind?!" he shouted furiously.

"I only wished to help you complete your collection, Master. Surely this will help in the next Shadow Games?"

"The Shadow Games don't matter right now. You stole from a demon even more powerful than Chaos himself. Do you realize that?"

"I knew this was gonna be good," Kryptone mused.

"No demon is stronger than Chaos, Master. Surely you understand that."

The Maker closed his eyes for a moment and took a deep breath to compose himself.

"If the rumors are to be believed, Chaos is one of two sons of Lucifer, you foolish waste of space!" he shouted. "Of course Lucifer would be an even worse demon!"

The Shadow was truly taken aback by this. This important information was something that he failed to obtain. It made him question his worth.

"You don't mean?" he processed, dumbfounded.

"Chaos is the demon of absolute darkness," the Maker said. "But he has another brother as well. Khais, demon of benevolence. He is the one who created this planet on which you stand, as well as the race of Immortals. With the intent of fighting off the angelic armies that fought against us. Both of them are supposedly children of Lucifer."

"I-I didn't realize," the Shadow stammered.

"Obviously not. Now we will have to prepare for the wrath of something even worse than a demon god. Begone from my fucking sight!"

"As you wish, Master," the Shadow replied, saddened.

The Shadow sank into the floor. His sadness was rather surprising. Shadows typically weren't capable of emotion. Pazuzu wandered over to the Maker.

"Are you alright, milord?" the elderly demon asked him.

The Maker gripped the arms of his chair tightly. The arms were cracking under his strength.

"Do I look like it?" the Maker growled.

"You will get through this," Pazuzu assured him. "You are an elder demon."

"Titles don't mean a thing," he replied. "Not when a demon like that wants you dead."

"Don't despair, milord. You still have your Shadow Games."

"I do enjoy the Shadow Games," he sighed. "I just don't know if there's any point to them now."

"The mortals would stand little chance of victory in your games, milord. They are brutal and gut-wrenching. You and I both know this."

The Maker considered this for a moment. While there was still a chance for the mortals to survive his games, there was also a greater chance that they could all perish in the process. He rather liked playing with the odds. This could end up being a gamble in his favor.

"Hmm," he pondered. "You may be right, Pazuzu. I'm glad that I keep you around."

"If the games fail to claim their lives, then I will do so in their stead," Pazuzu promised.

The Maker stood up and faced the chair he had once cherished.

"No, Pazuzu," he said quietly with a sinister tone. "If my games betray me, I will kill them myself."

"Fair enough, milord," Pazuzu said, bowing.

The Maker stretched out his hand, and dark energy swirled in the air. The energy had changed into a large battle hammer adorned with spikes. A skull's face was branded onto the center of the hammer's head. This was his favored weapon from all the ones that he could create at will. He gripped the handle of the hammer so tightly that his hands seemed to become pale.

Then he swung the hammer fiercely into his favorite chair. He just kept swinging into the chair, watching as it was destroyed under his unrelenting strikes. He screamed in frustration and didn't stop until the chair was nothing more than a broken heap on the ground in front of him. He breathed heavily, as he had put everything he had into the destruction of the chair in front of him.

"You heroes think you're so clever," he panted. "You killed the one demon that I considered to be my own brother. I will **never** forgive you for what you have done."

"Think that's our cue to leave," Kryptone said in a state of shock.

He guided Zigrone into the twisting halls of the arena. Even Pazuzu appeared surprised.

"Are you sure you're alright, milord?" Pazuzu asked worriedly.

The Maker turned to face him with beads of sweat trailing down his face, still breathing heavily.

"Shadow!" the Maker shouted.

The Shadow reappeared without hesitation.

"Find Roy and his merry band of misfits and do whatever it takes to lure them here," he said. "We only need one of these so-called noble heroes. They will surely come for whoever you take. Then once they all gather, I will crush them all at once."

"Of course, Master," the Shadow said, bowing. He dissipated into a miasma of darkness.

"Now tell our prisoners the good news," the Maker said, turning towards Pazuzu.

"What news is that, milord?" Pazuzu asked him.

"They finally have their chance at their freedom," he said. "They will be part of the Shadow Games, and if they do well enough, I may be gracious enough to free them."

"Of course, milord."

Pazuzu hobbled down the stairs into the twisting corridors of the arena. The Maker watched him go and stared down at the remains of his chair. He clenched his hands into tight fists.

"It is time to break Roy Darsetts physically and spiritually. He will learn what happens to those stupid enough to piss off an elder demon."

Pazuzu had been joined by several Archdemons as he made his way down the passage that led to their prisoners. He stopped at their cells. Vulcan was gripping the iron bars of his cell. He didn't recognize the elderly demon standing in front of him. He never came down here. He would see the demons often, but not one like him. The appearance of Pazuzu wandering down these halls was surprising, and he was far from friendly.

"Today's your lucky day, prisoners," Pazuzu said. "You will become part of my master's Shadow Games. A great honor for all who participate. Do well enough, and maybe you will be rid of this place."

"Truly?" Vulcan asked him hopefully.

"That is my master's decision," he replied. "Not mine."

Pazuzu snapped his fingers, and the Archdemons unlocked the cells.

"Try anything funny, and I will not hesitate to kill you all," Pazuzu warned.

The four of them grabbed their weapons and followed the demons out into the now cramped hallway. Pazuzu's old and decrepit hand rested on the hilt of the large, bandaged sword on his back as they walked. He gave off the visage of an elderly demon. Dragos arched his spear towards the old demon in front of them. Arthur grabbed his spear by the long handle.

"Don't even try it, Dragos," Arthur whispered in his ear. "He is a lot stronger than he appears."

"What are you even talking about?" Dragos whispered in a grunt of displeasure.

"I can see his hidden aura," Aeolia confirmed in his other ear. "His dark aura is overwhelming. His very body is bound to the dark soul contained within that blade strapped to his back. He is at that sword's mercy. Probably why he walks in such an odd way."

Dragos sighed. Of course it wouldn't be that easy. They reached a heavy metallic door, and everyone stopped. An Archdemon grabbed the door handle and swung it open. Its bottom scraped against the cavern floor. An earsplitting screech echoed around them as the door slid across the floor. The prisoners cringed at the shrill echo.

"Get inside," Pazuzu ordered. "Next time that door opens, the Shadow Games will have begun."

"So, you brought us out of our separate cells just to toss us into a new one?" Vulcan asked.

"Just get inside," the elderly demon growled. "Before I lose my patience."

The four of them made their way into the room that the demons had made for them. There wasn't much in the room. A shabby metal table and chairs sat in the center of the room. A few barrels were pressed up against the corners of the room. A dimly lit light bulb dangled loosely over the table. That's all they really had to look forward to.

The heavy door was slammed shut, and they unwillingly had the screeching noise piercing their eardrums for a second time. Then the light was all but blotted out. If not for the pitiful light bulb, it would have been even more dreadful.

"This is a fine mess that we're in," Vulcan said.

"You're the one who had to open your damned mouth!" Dragos shot back.

"His actions wouldn't have changed anything," Arthur said, looking around the gloomy room. "They would have put us here regardless. This was always their plan. Keep us here and force us to fight horrific monsters in front of a crowd of demons."

"How do you know so much about all this?" Vulcan asked.

"I have been watching them carefully," he replied. "Listened in on some of their conversations. The demons don't hide things very well. If you had been listening, you would have heard it too."

Vulcan felt that he was probably right. He had spent so much time trying to get out of his cell, he hadn't considered anything else. His focus had been too narrow.

"Looks like now we wait," Vulcan sighed.

"Now we wait," Arthur agreed.

***

Pazuzu took the long, twisting paths back up to the place where the Maker awaited him. His master still stood at the pile of rubble, staring at it, deep in thought. Baelor's death had taken quite the toll on him.

"It is done, milord," Pazuzu declared, grabbing the Maker's attention.

"Excellent, Pazuzu," the Maker said. "Then very soon the Shadow Games will begin anew with the most epic battles this place has ever seen. Our honorable guests will be the stars of the show. Soon they will be introduced to the hordes of demons waiting outside in anticipation."

"I'm sure they will be the best Shadow Games yet, milord."

The Maker turned towards Pazuzu, grinning ear to ear. "I can't wait for the fear they will bear as they are shown how cruel I can be. They will pay dearly for what they did to my precious brother, Baelor."

"I look forward to it, milord."

The Maker continued grinning maliciously and laughed maniacally into the air.

"Your time is coming to an end, mortals!" he declared.

# THE END